QUARREL WITH THE FOE

Mel Bradshaw

RENDEZVOUS PRESS

Cover art: Franklin Carmichael / Library and Archives Canada C-130431

RendezVous Press acknowledges the support of the Canada Council for our publishing program.

Published by Napoleon Publishing / RendezVous Press
Toronto, Ontario, Canada
www.rendezvouspress.com

09 08 07 06 05   5 4 3 2 1

Library and Archives Canada Cataloguing in Publication

Bradshaw, Mel, date
Quarrel with the foe / Mel Bradshaw.

ISBN 1-894917-28-6

I. Title.

PS8603.R332Q37 2005   C813'.6   C2005-903470-X

For my brothers Bill and Jim

&

To the memory of our parents

Ruth Anne Harris (1903-1968) and

Melville Alexander Bradshaw (1898-1974)

Take up our quarrel with the foe:
To you from failing hands we throw
The torch; be yours to hold it high.
If ye break faith with us who die
We shall not sleep, though poppies grow
In Flanders fields.

—John McCrae

Curtain-Raiser

Yeah, I was at the battery that May afternoon when Horny Ingersoll had everything between his legs cut away by a piece of exploding field gun. When he hooked on the lanyard and gave it a pull, the breech block just flew apart. Even the gunners were stunned by the noise. The officer had telephoned for high explosive shells, and it was beyond miraculous none of the rest of us was hurt.

I was just a tourist, come over to see what Horny and his pals thought they were doing for us foot soldiers. Horny and I had been back and forth all the summer before as to which service we'd enlist in. Horny's dad was all for the guns, thought they were more manly, and he bullied us both hard. He was a rough-tongued, angry man, who kept harking back to something he'd read about "C" Battery and the Relief of Mafeking. In the end, Horny saw things his way, and I—for reasons no better and now forgotten—was stubborn enough to choose a highland regiment of infantry.

I'd have felt the breeze if I'd been wearing my kilt that day.

I was out of the line, but I'd just been through a hot time in the Salient, and my nerves were still pretty taut. Almost before the 18-pounder exploded, I'd dived into the gunners' dug-out and was looking for a stretcher. Nothing doing—but the table was an old door lying unsecured on top of various crates. Sending ration tins flying, I hauled this door up and out to where the bombardier was trying to make the small first aid dressing we all carried stop the bleeding from a very big wound. I passed him the dressing from my kit as well. Unwinding Horny's puttees from around his shins, I handed one to the other fellow and together we tied the dressings on as best we could. Then we lifted Horny onto the door and tied him to that.

It was a long two thousand yards back to the wagon lines. I was short of breath and still coughing quite a bit from the gassing I'd got. The combined weight of Horny and those planks must have been considerable, but what you noticed most was the difficulty of keeping the door level. I was carrying the back, so that responsibility fell mostly to me. A big gunner, six foot four if an inch, was on the front, where he didn't have to look. Whatever thoughts I could spare from the balancing act, as I watched Horny's blood soak through the khaki cloth bindings, were for how I'd known Horny since before he'd debauched his first maiden and how we'd now have to find him another nickname.

We didn't though. He had lost too much blood. We buried him at the dressing station, and Horner C. Ingersoll is what the War Graves Commission eventually carved on his headstone beneath the maple leaf. He was holding my hand when he died. I think I'd meant just to shake hands, but he didn't want to let go, and when I felt the pressure—panicky hard at first, but weakening with every passing second, damned if I wanted to let go either. In less than another minute, it was all over.

I hadn't much stomach for going back up to the gun pits after that, but it seemed unfriendly to let the big gunner go alone. So off we trudged. Horny's crew no longer had a gun to fire, and we found them cleaning up as best they could before some brass hat put them to work elsewhere.

I didn't know their surnames, then. They'd been introduced to me as Sam, the bombardier, Ivan, and

Tinker, also called Bobbie—my fellow stretcher-bearer. There should have been one more private, but he had been decapitated by a German whizz-bang the night before and hadn't yet been replaced. When Tinker and I got back, Ivan was reading out what was stamped on one of the H. E. shell casings—Peerless Armaments, Hamilton.

"Let me see that round," said Sam. "Hamilton, no guff. Whosoever's company that is, I bet he's making a fortune sending us these darlings."

"Think I'll look him up," said Ivan, "if I get out of this alive."

"If the Boche win the war," said Tinker, "they'll be giving him a sodding medal."

"I'll give him something to pin on his chest," said Ivan. He had his clasp knife out and was flicking it open and closed.

"On his chest or a little lower down," said Sam. "Look at this, would you?" He was poking a needle or straight pin into the casing of the eighteen-pound shell. "This metal is full of holes. The bastards just filled them in with paint so the rounds would pass inspection."

"That's a new one." Ivan caught one of the crumbs of pigment on the end of a finger and studied it closely. "Christ," he said, pressing down on every word, "are all the circles of hell taken?"

I felt a cough coming, which I tried to squelch so as not to draw any questions my way.

"Ha—ah—hack! hack!"

"What about you, Paul?" asked Tinker. "You knew Horny longer than any of us. Bet you wouldn't mind getting Mr. Peerless in a dark alley."

"No," I said, "I wouldn't."

I could hear my voice sounded strained. And to be frank, I felt put in a false position. Yes, I had been to school with Horny, and to his home for that matter, but we hadn't been truly close. As I say, I came to see him mainly to watch the guns at work. Length of acquaintance didn't seem to matter that much compared to what Horny and these men had been through together. To face death beside another for as little as a week means more than sitting in the same schoolroom for five years.

I liked Horny well enough, and we'd roughhoused together, but I hadn't kept up with him once girls entered the picture. I had been a late developer, not one of the fast set.

Still, I didn't want to tell the gunners any of this. It would have been disloyal. Horny had been a good soldier, as far as I knew, and had met a rotten fate at the hands of his own country's arms-makers. At the time, I didn't even know if there was a single owner behind Peerless Armaments. One thing for sure: if there was one, he had not deliberately blown Horny apart. He might not even have given the order to paint over the holes in the metal. On the other hand, he was employing and letting himself be enriched by fraud artists of the most despicable stripe. On that spring day in 1915 outside Ypres, while I listened to Sam, Tinker and Ivan bragging about settling scores, there was one word I couldn't get out of my head—manslaughter. The slaughter of men as if they were cattle, with no malice—without even the limited malice combatants reserved for opposing armies—but carelessly, wantonly.

I knew that the peacetime criminal code did not prescribe capital punishment for that offence—but since coming to Europe, I'd seen too many soldiers let down by Canadian suppliers, cheated by compatriots who risked nothing. Under the circumstances, I thought executing the bosses—a quick and merciful execution by firing squad—sounded pretty reasonable.

Chapter One

I wasn't on duty the night Digby Watt was found lying "in the gutter" in front of his office with a fatal dose of lead in his chest. He was found by a journalist who claimed to have been tipped off by an anonymous phone call at around one forty-five a.m. The journalist's name was Ivan MacAllister. The date was April 20, 1926.

I first read about it in the newspaper when I got to police headquarters later that morning. The article ended jarringly with the words, "Who's next?" I accompanied my reading with a cup of coffee and a handful of Aspirins. I had a rather severe morning-after headache, something an enforcer of the Ontario Temperance Act could scarcely admit to.

Especially not with Detective Inspector Sanderson looming over my desk.

"Shameful journalism," said Sanderson. "What business has that rag asking who's next as if this were the start of a bloodbath?"

It was easy to imagine the inspector in a clerical collar, fixing a congregation with that blue glare under a straight-across hedge of black eyebrow. The high, broad forehead above only added weight to the disapproval. I knew, though, there was something more. A connection by marriage to the publisher of the *Toronto Examiner* had made the two men dogged rivals.

"All that fear-mongering does is put my detectives under

pressure to do a rush job." Sanderson papered over the newsprint on my desk with official documents as he spoke. "Get busy, Paul. I want you to read the reports of the investigating constable and the medical examiner. Then go round to the house and interview the family. There's the son Morris who worked with Watt, and Morris's wife. Also an unmarried daughter, Edith."

"Sure thing. But won't Mr. Fergus's nose be put out of joint if a whipper-snapper like me gets first crack at the genteel folk?" Wilf Fergus at age sixty-three was the city's senior detective sergeant and let no one, including the slightly younger inspector, forget it.

"Fergus is indisposed." A twitch of the eyebrow hedge warned me off asking for specifics. "So—I'm giving youth a chance. I assume in your officers' mess they taught you something of polite society."

"I'll try to keep my boots off the furniture."

"Never mind Watt's business associates: Knight and one of the acting detectives are talking to them—lad named Cruickshank from Station Number One if you need him for anything. And never mind looking for eyewitnesses. I've a couple more men doing that thankless job. Better see Watt's fiancée, though, if that's what she was."

"Fiancée?" I hadn't come across that in my reading. "Digby's?"

"The children's mother died two years ago. My wife tells me there's gossip about a younger woman, much younger. Get her name from that journalist MacAllister. You should speak to him anyway. On your way now, and, Paul..."

"Yes, boss?"

"I don't like my men drinking, even on their own time. You don't have to be angelic, but you do have to be alert."

"I'll be both, sir."

I sorted the documents I'd been given into piles. I continued sorting even after Sanderson had withdrawn and had turned his searching gaze on some other sinner. While this wasn't my first homicide assignment, it was the first time I'd been asked to interview the principals on my own. It was an occasion, if hardly one for butterflies in the stomach. Despite my inspector's reference to giving youth a chance, I was well into my thirties and past all that.

I tackled the constable's report first. He had arrived at 96 Adelaide Street West at 2:33 a.m. in response to a telephone call from Ivan MacAllister, of Broadview Avenue, who remained on the scene. Also present when the police arrived was Morris Watt of Glen Road. There, in front of a six-storey office block, had been found the body of a grey-haired male in his sixties lying face up on the sidewalk. Not, as MacAllister reported, in the gutter, but with his head pointed that way, which suggested he had been facing the building when he fell. The constable had neglected to include a sketch with his report. The deceased was identified by Morris as his father Digby Watt. There was wet blood on the jacket and vest, apparently proceeding from three separate gunshot wounds. On closer inspection, it was found that only two bullets had penetrated the deceased's chest, the third lodging harmlessly in *Daily Strength for Daily Needs*, a leather-bound volume nestled in his left inside jacket pocket. This bullet, although deformed by the impact, was judged to be point two-five calibre. No firearm was found at the scene, nor any cartridge cases. The deceased's wallet was in his pocket and contained ninety-seven dollars. The deceased's fly was open, and the penis and testicles pulled out in full view.

I sat up when I read that. The *Examiner* stated only that

Watt's clothing had been "disarranged" and that he had been left "partially naked".

At 2:45 a.m., the constable used the pay phone at Sheppard Street and Adelaide to summon the medical examiner, who arrived at 3:28 a.m. Based on a temperature reading, the medical examiner estimated the body had been cooling for between one and two hours, placing the time of death between 1:30 and 2:30 a.m. He gave the opinion that the two wounds were most consistent with small calibre bullets fired from the front. Death would have resulted immediately. No other marks of violence were discovered. There were no apparent exit wounds, so an autopsy ought to be able to recover the two unaccounted-for projectiles. In accordance with police practice, these would be sent over to the University of Toronto for ballistic analysis. The deceased had been taken to Grace Hospital at College and Huron Streets for further post-mortem examination.

I rubbed my temples, then picked a nickel from my right side trouser pocket. Heads I'd go to Glen Road first, tails to the newspaper offices. It was a good throw, the coin rocketing straight and high and executing many revolutions before plopping comfortably into the palm of my hand. I slapped it onto the back of my left wrist.

The king's bearded profile.

I picked up the telephone and asked for the number of the *Toronto Examiner*. I'd never let chance rule my life more than was necessary and wasn't about to start. Ivan MacAllister was the first person on the scene and that made him the person to start with. As luck would have it, he was still in the office.

"Wait till I get there," I told him.

I unlocked the right top drawer of my desk. There,

wrapped in its shoulder strap, lay my slate-grey service revolver. The Webley Mark IV, while smaller than the bulky Mark VI lugged about by British officers during the war, was a weight all the same and helped not at all with most detective work. I closed the drawer again and locked the pistol inside. Having already endured my morning visit from the inspector, I decided that today—in defiance of regulations—I'd chance going without.

Headquarters of the Toronto Police Department occupied a cramped suite on the ground floor of City Hall, so cramped that a couple of desks had been pushed out into the wide hall. There a pair of self-conscious clerks drew up their reports in guiltless exile. I envied them, especially on head-sore mornings, and renewed my standing offer of a desk swap when the click of my heels made them look up. The dim corridors with their cool tiles made for a soothing middle ground between the chaos of the office and the chaos of the town. When I got out, too soon, onto the soot-darkened rose sandstone front steps and looked down Bay Street, I couldn't see Lake Ontario for the new elevated railway tracks feeding into the perpetually under-construction new Union Station. The street teemed with billboards, shop signs, streetcar wires, square black Ford motor cars, jaywalkers in flapping spring overcoats, and a lone traffic cop, straight and tall in his English-bobby style helmet. Him I did not envy.

In sympathy, I took my own hat off and carried it. The morning was overcast, but mild and dry. Truth to tell, there wasn't a lot of difference between outdoors and the office. The street smelled of traffic, not spring flowers. Doubtless it was the sort of day Digby Watt would have liked. A good day for business in that it did not immediately distract the susceptible with memories of springtime romance, or the more prosaic with thoughts of the golf course.

Digby Watt had rarely been distracted by any sort of weather or any normal notion of quitting time. At age sixty-seven, he had been notorious for staying at his office past midnight. It would not have been difficult for anyone who wanted him dead to find him on a dark and lonely street, empty as only a street in the financial district can be at that hour.

Despite the traffic, it took me no more than five minutes to walk from Queen and Bay to the *Examiner* Building, a squat four-storey block on King Street West. The commissionaire told me I'd find MacAllister on the second floor, turn right at the first landing and ask anyone in the city room.

The room contained a scattering of eight or ten reporters working candlestick phones rather than pounding the pavement. Some were bleary-eyed veterans who looked even more hung over than I felt, some teenaged cubs in their first pair of long pants. I overheard one of the latter commiserating with a man over the death of his pet monkey and asking for the juicy particulars that might pump readers' tear ducts or jiggle their funny bone.

They all looked far too industrious to interrupt, but in the end I didn't have to ask. I recognized my man across the room as the Ivan who had worked the same field gun in Flanders as my former classmate Horny Ingersoll.

Ivan had remained long and thin, with small thin hands I could still see flicking a clasp knife open and shut. Right at this moment, he was playing rummy for cigarettes with one of the women reporters. He had apparently made it through the war and into gainful employment with four limbs and two eyes intact. He had grown a thin, mud-coloured moustache that somehow went with the sneering expression successful newsmen are supposed to have. His brown tweeds could have leaped from the day's fashion page—loose in the trousers, tight in the sleeves, with four buttons at each cuff. He was easily the best-dressed person in sight.

He'd spotted me right away and, without neglecting the hand he was playing, kept track of my approach, though he wasn't able to place me until I reminded him we'd met before.

"Sure enough. Horny's pal." A smile broke from under the moustache and he stuck out his hand. "Lulu, your revenge will have to wait."

Lulu moved off with a wistful look back at a hard-earned quarter's worth of smokes she was leaving on Ivan's blotter.

Ivan's grip was firm, his fingers slender but strong. The finger tips were stained nicotine brown.

"What brings you here?" A half-smoked cigarette between his lips wobbled as he spoke.

I showed my wallet badge. "Digby Watt."

"A copper!" Ivan looked me up and down more closely, evidently thinking of a newspaperly way to describe my un-ironed suit, red eyes, and badly shaved chin. "Maybe that figures. I think you impressed us at the battery as a tough guy who listens more than he talks."

I shrugged.

"Still," Ivan continued, "aren't you about ten years too young to be a detective sergeant?"

Not wanting to start an argument, at least not yet, I omitted to point out that (a) I was the youngest police officer of my rank by only four years, (b) I wasn't a total upstart as I had been on the force before the war, and (c) I could be garrulous enough when not witnessing the intimate mutilation of a childhood playmate. What I did say was—

"Looks like you're not doing badly yourself. You have a private office where we can go and get away from these jabbering Teletype machines?"

"You're a scream. And don't tell me you have a private office back at City Hall, or I'll think I've missed my calling."

I threw my weight around and got a junior editor to yield up his glassed-in cubicle on the south side of the building. The sun was coming out over the lake and the room was too hot. I loosened my tie and, pushing some papers aside, sat on the edge of the desk. Ivan took a wooden arm chair and lit a fresh cigarette off the butt of its predecessor.

"You got a phone call late last night?" I began.

"At 1:45. Have you read my article? It's all in there." Ivan wasn't irritated, not yet. You just got the feeling that he was intrigued by the unexpected meeting and would rather have talked about old times and old acquaintance.

"Did you check the time?" I asked, dutifully but mechanically. For my mind also was going back to that afternoon before Ypres.

"I checked the time."

"Ivan," I said, "how much did you know about Digby Watt before last night?"

"Lots. I'd be no good at my job if I didn't. Big man on Bay Street *without* being larger than life. Came up through commerce and finance. No factory experience. Has a reputation for character rather than personality. Cheerful and humourless. A ready smile, but no wit or appreciation of wit in others. Saw *The Gold Rush* and didn't laugh. Generous with money, close with information, protective of women, and appealing to women that like to be protected. But I think you're asking when I found out who owned Peerless Armaments during the period they were killing our gunners with bum shells."

"Well?"

"Don't remember. Years ago."

"O-kay. Do you live alone?"

Ivan hesitated.

"Yeah," he said. "Over a sporting goods store, just north of the Danforth. But if you're thinking there was no call at 1:45, the phone company will tell you otherwise."

"Did anyone else see or hear you take the call?"

"At that hour? No, no one. I have my own telephone in the apartment. Sometimes the paper calls me late, so it's worth it."

"You were asleep?"

"Yeah."

"Was the caller male or female?"

"A man."

"Did you recognize the voice? Or is there any voice you've heard since that you recognize as that of the caller?"

"No and no."

Ivan sounded relaxed, resigned now to being questioned. I dug my notebook out of an inside jacket pocket.

"I'd like to hear how the conversation went. Word for word."

"Ring-ring. 'Hello.' 'Ivan MacAllister?' 'Yeah; who's this?' 'Is Ivan a foreign name?' 'Not in my case. What is this about?' 'Ninety-six Adelaide West. You won't be sorry.' Before I could say anything more, he hung up."

I wrote. "That's everything? You're certain?"

"No guff—that's it."

"Anything there to suggest the caller's identity? The foreign-name business, say."

"I get that sometimes. It would have been worse if my parents had got really cute and called me Siegfried."

Worse during the war, I thought. By now red Russians were overtaking Jerry in the sweepstakes of villainy. I let it drop.

"What did you do after he hung up?" I asked.

"Lit a smoke and grumbled to myself that it was probably some crank who didn't like the way I wrote, but while I was grumbling, I was getting dressed and calling for a taxi. The newshound who can pass up a potential scoop might as well hand in his company pencil."

"What time did you get to 96 Adelaide West?"

"About two fifteen."

"By that watch?"

"Sure. Did you want to look at it?" Ivan let his cigarette dangle from his lips as he unstrapped the Bulova from his wrist.

It occurred to me that, although Ivan was likely a heavy smoker, too many of his fingers were brown for the stains to be nicotine. What else could they be?

I took Ivan's watch and noted that it was two minutes faster than my own. Mine was likely the one in error, though; Ivan's was the better watch, and how! A gift perhaps, or the symptom of a second job. But, if neither, if a crime columnist earned enough to be buying Bulovas, Ivan wasn't the one in the wrong racket.

"Have you reset it since?"

"Never needs it."

"So you reached the address indicated by two fifteen. Fast work."

"I was lucky. The car came pronto."

"Would you have its number?"

"Didn't notice, but it was a Danforth Dollar Taxi. They'll find the driver for you."

"And was Digby Watt lying dead on the sidewalk when you got there?"

"Sure, just as I wrote."

"Come on, Ivan," I said. "Journalism's show business. And showmen have to pep facts up or, in this case, tone them down to make a picture that thrills the Sunday school teachers but doesn't shock them. When you and I are talking, I'd never hold you to what you write to earn your pay."

"Calling my work hokum, Paul?" Calm still, but less agreeable.

"For instance," I said, "you ask, 'Who's next?' Do you have any reason to believe the killer will strike again?"

"I figured if a man as established as that could be shot down on his doorstep, no one's safe."

"And I guess you always want to give folks a reason to buy tomorrow's paper." No reaction from Ivan, so I carried on. "Did the caller say anything on the phone, or was there anything at the crime scene to indicate there would be further victims?"

"Neither."

"And you found Watt just as you write?"

"He was dead when I got there. I didn't move him."

"Did you touch him?"

"To see if he needed a doctor and an ambulance—sure. He didn't. What he needed was the police, so I called you."

"What about the son, Morris Watt? Was he there when you arrived?"

"He showed up four or five minutes later. He'd been working late with the old man, but he'd gone to get the car from a parking garage. Digby must have been standing waiting for him when someone popped him."

"Let me get this straight: while you were looking the body over, Morris showed up in Watt's car."

"On foot. He said he couldn't get the car started. Once he arrived, I went to phone the police."

"And how did Morris take his father's death?"

"Noisily. 'This can't be true! This is terrible! If only the car had been working, I'd have been back in time.' Stuff like that."

"So, you were alone with the senior Watt for five minutes. Did you recognize him?"

"Sure. I work for a paper. He gets his picture in the paper."

"Take any pictures last night?" I asked.

"The *Examiner* employs me as a writer, not a photographer. And they don't print pictures of deaders, even fully clothed. You can take that as no."

Something warned me not to, but I couldn't pin it down.

"Ivan, who's this girl Watt was stepping out with?"

"You'd have to ask the guy that writes the Evy Chatters column. He's not in the office."

"Was Watt engaged?"

"Search me."

The sunlight and the smoke from his cigarette were making Ivan squint, which shrunk his already small eyes down to hairline cracks, but I could still see in them a gleam of superiority. He wasn't altogether enjoying himself, but he still thought he was handling himself well, could perhaps handle any bull's questions with his brain on two-thirds power.

"When Horny died," I let fall, "you said you thought you'd look up the man behind Peerless Armaments if you got through the war. Did you ever meet Digby Watt while he was alive?"

"Not once."

"How come? You did say you thought you'd look him up."

Ivan stood up and towered over me.

"Now you're making me sore, Paul. You'd take what a soldier on the battlefield says when he's just lost a pal, and you'd put it in a police file? Not only is that a dirty trick, it's a dumb one—and I took you for a smarter guy than that. You were there, weren't you? You must know that just to keep some shred of sanity men let off steam by saying any number of things. But by the time we came home, the last thing we wanted was to settle old scores. I'd no interest in meeting up with Watt. He was a business story, and I was on the crime beat. To hell with him."

"Sounds to me like you're still mad at him. Was his clothing disarranged when you got there?"

"No, but I just never could resist petting stiffs."

With that, Ivan strode out of the small office and disappeared behind the stairwell door. It was a fine exit, and I decided not to ruin it by giving chase.

Chapter Two

Before leaving the editor's private office, I picked up his telephone and asked for an outside line. When I rang Bell and gave them my badge number, they were able to confirm one call from a public booth on the west side of Sheppard Street to the Broadview Avenue home of subscriber I. A. MacAllister, which call commenced at 1:44 a.m. and lasted less than a minute. Also a call at 1:51 of similar duration from MacAllister's residence to the Danforth Dollar Taxi Service. As they had informed me often enough before, the phone company had no record of the content of these conversations or the identity of the parties involved. I always asked, ever hopeful as well as fearful about the progress of snooping.

My next call was to Danforth Dollar Taxi. They claimed to have received a request for a car at 1:51 from a man calling himself Ivan MacAllister. Driver Tony Bellotto promptly proceeded from the company depot at Danforth and Pape to 786 Broadview Avenue and at 2:01 picked up a fare identifying himself as Ivan MacAllister. Said fare was let off at 96 Adelaide Street West at 2:14.

Sounded like speeding, but let that go.

Yet another phone call revealed Morris Watt to be at the office rather than at home, so I deferred the pleasure of a visit to Glen Road. From the Examiner Building up to 96 Adelaide West was too short a stroll to allow for heavy-duty thinking. Instead, I gawked like any rube at all the construction. Since well before the war, Toronto had been putting up skyscrapers with as many as twelve or fifteen floors, but even downtown these towers were still the exception. Four storeys was about as high as you could go without attracting attention or requiring an elevator. Watt's building had six.

It was on the north side of the street, and the patch of pavement where Digby Watt had fallen was bathed in sunshine. No blood had spilled onto the concrete. There was nothing to mark the spot. The sight of brogues and oxfords, pumps and workboots tramping over it held me a moment, fascinated. It put me in mind of a phrase beloved of military chaplains, something about this being the way worldly glory passes. Pedestrian traffic was certainly picking up as the City Hall clock struck noon. Men in suits were on the march from their offices to their clubs, while their secretaries trotted off to the sandwich shops to pick up something they could take back to their desks. A couple of bank branches and a shoe repair were also pulling in their share of lunch-hour traffic. It would be a lonely street at night, though. No theatres or cinemas, no houses or apartments. No late night cafés. If you shot someone here after midnight with a modest-sized gun, you wouldn't even need a silencer.

I stepped briefly around the corner of the building onto Sheppard Street to have a look at the phone from which someone had called Ivan's apartment at 1:44. There was nothing much to see, just an ordinary wooden phone booth with a black coin-phone inside. I poked around the gum wrappers on the floor to see if our caller might have left something personal behind—a hand-written note would have been swell—but there was nothing doing. It was too late to have the handset dusted for fingerprints. It had been too late at 2:45 a.m., the moment the constable had used this phone to call in the medical examiner instead of taking the two dozen extra steps to the nearest police call box. I reminded myself that constables weren't trained or paid enough to worry about such things. But why had there been no detective on the scene?

I tightened my necktie and went back to Adelaide Street and in through the double brass doors of number 96.

From the directory in the lobby, it was clear to any reader of the financial pages that every occupant had something to do with the Watt business empire, yet neither the building itself nor any of the individual concerns bore his name. Atkins Hardware headed the list, followed by Beaconsfield Power, Canada Ski and Snowshoe, and so down through the alphabet. "P" was represented by Peerless Kitchen Appliances. Unlike the Examiner Building, 96 Adelaide had no concierge or commissionaire to make enquiries of, and I was momentarily at a loss as to how to find my man Morris. If I had to guess, I thought I'd take a chance on Dominion Consolidated Holdings, which had a certain managerial ring. Suite 402.

When the elevator came down and deposited another clutch of lunch-goers in the lobby, the operator was able to confirm my choice. He was a man of about my age with black hair slicked straight back like a jazz-band player and a right arm that ended above the elbow. I thought it would have been more convenient for him to turn about, but he plainly preferred not to unsettle his passengers by staring at them and reached across his body with his left hand to operate the controls. On arrival at the fourth floor, I did not get out right away.

"Were you on duty last night when Mr. Digby Watt left the building?"

Turning, the operator saw the police identification I was holding up. "I leave at six, sir, and come back on at eight in the morning."

"How many times in a normal week would he stay later than six?"

"He was always in before I got here and after I left. The only time I'd see him would be when he had an outside appointment during the day."

I saw the car was rated for a maximum of twelve passengers.

"Would you," I asked, "always notice when he rode with you?"

"Notice?" The man's grin showed a mouthful of tobacco-stained teeth. "He never rode with me without speaking to me, no matter who he was with. And it wasn't just the 'How are you, Harold?' you get from people who couldn't care less. Usually, he'd ask me about the hockey game, but if we were alone in the car he might try to persuade me to let him fit me out with some new artificial arm he'd heard about. I always told him I'd rather not, unless he thought a war amputee made people uncomfortable and was bad for business. 'Not a bit of it,' he'd say. 'Harold, you did the Empire proud in France, and I don't care who knows it.'"

The car was being summoned to the sixth floor.

"You'll miss him, Harold," I said.

The operator's mouth tightened. "I thought we were through having good men shot. Hope you get the S.O.B. that did it."

The fourth-floor receptionist, a grey-haired woman in pince-nez spectacles, sat behind a desk loaded with communication equipment, including a wax-cylinder Dictaphone and an intercom of the speaker and mike variety. I was surprised when instead of using the latter to announce my arrival she rose from her place, puffing a little as if her corset were laced too tight.

She showed me into a well-equipped office of modest dimensions and austere decor. Mushroom-grey would have been too garish a description of the wall colour. The window faced north and was covered by a Venetian blind, closed plainly more for privacy than shade. A second door stood open, revealing an office slightly larger and even less excitingly furnished.

The desk immediately before me was in fact a rather handsome cherrywood, and something told me I wouldn't be plunking my derrière on its polished surface. On the far side of it, a thirtyish man with dark wavy hair looked up from a pile of telegrams, presumably of condolence. As his baby-blue eyes registered my presence, he passed his hand over the lower part of his face in a reflexive gesture of pain, then rose with a quite creditable smile of welcome.

"Morris Watt," he said, coming round the desk and shaking my hand. "And you'll be Detective Sergeant Shenstone. Please sit down."

The armchair indicated was comfortable, but of the sort you'd find at the head of a dining room table. I was green enough in the ways of plutocrats to be expecting something plusher, more like the bloated bum rests of a hotel lounge or C.P.R. parlour car. While settling in, I noticed in a yellow metal frame on a side wall a recent studio photograph of Morris's late father; he was smiling slightly but already in life somewhat sepulchral on account of the almost bald head and the dark skin under dark, deep-set eyes. I suspected that even a picture of Digby taken at Morris's current age would show the son to be the handsomer of the two. The planes of Morris's face came together in the way sculptors seemed to find congenial when portraying an idealized volunteer to adorn a war memorial. The vertical depression running from his nose to the middle of his upper lip was particularly pronounced in a way that suggested seriousness of character.

"How can I help you, Mr. Shenstone?" Morris had pushed his own chair back from his interrupted reading and was now sitting with his hands folded on his crossed legs. He looked neither nervous nor, despite his prompt, impatient. I was having some difficulty hearing in my mind's ear the distraught ejaculations Ivan MacAllister had reported.

"Was it your father's custom to work late here at the office?"

"Yes. Much more so since my mother's death. That was two years ago now."

"And did you usually stay and work with him?"

"Not every night. He was aware that, unlike him, I had a wife waiting up for me. But I was always with him when he intended to stay past eleven p.m. Then he felt it would be too late to ask Curtis to pick him up."

"His chauffeur?"

"Oh, yes. Excuse me."

"He never drove himself?"

"He didn't drive, no." Morris smiled. "Though Curtis did offer to teach him."

"So on the nights when he was staying past eleven, where did you park the car?"

"Braddock's Garage on Pearl Street. Do you know it?"

"Just west of York." I remembered a one-storey building accommodating an automobile livery and repair service. Parking by the day or the month was available on the flat roof. "The car was out of doors then?"

"Yes, but at least it was off the street."

"The traffic police approve of that," I assured him. "On the nights the car was parked at Braddock's, Mr. Watt, did your father usually accompany you from the office to the garage when it was time to go home?"

"If he had, none of this would have happened!" Morris exclaimed peevishly.

Now it starts, I thought. This crying over spilt milk was presumably what Ivan had heard a lot of the night before.

"You can't be sure of that, sir," I said. "In any case, it was your father's practice to wait on the sidewalk while you got the car. Correct?"

"In winter or if it was raining, he might wait inside the foyer till he saw me pull up. But in clement weather—"

"He waited outside," I supplied. "How long did it take you from the moment you left him till the moment you returned with the car?"

"Never longer than five minutes. I can answer that with certainty because I often timed myself. Five minutes was the maximum until last night. Then last night the car... What a nightmare!"

"The car wouldn't start?"

"It started all right, but before I got it down the ramp and out onto the street, at the first turn in fact, the steering gear failed. I knew right away that it would take some time to repair and that I had no hope of finding a mechanic between two and three in the morning. The thing to do was to call a cab and get my father home. So I made for a public telephone."

"There was no one downstairs in the garage, no night watchman?"

"No. The only security at night is provided by a padlocked chain across the ramp. People who rent parking space by the month are given a key."

"Which phone did you use, the one at Adelaide and Sheppard?"

"I knew the closest booth was just south of the garage, on King, so that's where I went, even though it took me farther afield. That was wrong. I should have gone back and told my father first. Then maybe..."

"You might only have got yourself shot too, sir. Did you in fact call a cab?"

"Yes, to meet me at 96 Adelaide West. And then I hurried back there."

"Last night the weather was good, so I presume you had left your father standing on the sidewalk."

"Yes, that's right."

"And do you know what time it was when you left him to get the car?"

"Not precisely. It must have been about two o'clock."

"Two?" Here was a surprise. If Ivan and Morris were both telling the truth, the journalist had been tipped off about the murder at least fifteen minutes before it happened. "Are you sure, Mr. Watt?"

"It must have been two. I had glanced at my watch at twenty to, and at that time we were still working on the annual report. I'd guess it took us twenty minutes from then to put away our papers and get downstairs."

"How long would you say it was then from the time you left your father until the time when you got back to the front entrance of the office building?"

"I checked my watch while phoning Platinum Taxi. It was eleven minutes past two then. I'd say I got back to where I'd left my father at two fifteen or a little later."

Morris used a fine old pocket watch rather than a wrist model. As I had with Ivan MacAllister, I checked the time currently indicated and got the owner's assurance that it hadn't been reset since the night before. My watch was running just under two minutes faster. I had no idea yet how crucial these stray minutes would turn out to be, but I was taking phone company time, which agreed with Danforth Dollar Taxi time, as the most reliable. Compared to that standard, Ivan's Bulova was a minute fast, my Waterbury a minute slow, and bringing up the rear at three minutes slow was Morris Watt's Heuer—which I noticed was engraved with his father's name: *To our dear son Digby on his 21st birthday*. A hand-me-down, in short.

"Mr. Watt," it occurred to me to ask, "what is your position at Dominion Consolidated Holdings?"

A new look of pain clouded the other man's face.

"I was being trained. You might say my position was 'the boss's son'."

"And how long was this training period?"

"Until my father thought I was ready for a more formal place in one of his concerns. Yesterday, he said he thought he'd have a place for me by September."

"Had he ever said something like that before, named a month?"

"Yes, but then he took his companies public, and all the work involved caused delays. He wanted to make sure I wasn't pushed ahead too fast only to fall on my face. I had to be able to go into a position and earn respect on my own, not just be tolerated because of my name."

This was gilding your fetters with a vengeance. In Morris's place, I'd have done a bunk for Australia—if only to keep from throttling dear old dad.

"And just when did this training position begin, Mr. Watt?" I asked.

"When I got discharged from the army in July 1919."

"A long apprenticeship." It wasn't a question.

"Does this have a bearing on your investigation, sergeant?"

I shrugged. My mouth was dry, and the sun was now well over the yard-arm. I debated with myself whether Morris might have a bottle somewhere for the entertainment of visitors. Digby Watt had been an unwavering prohibitionist. Was there enough rebel spirit or enough cunning in the son to conceal a rum ration under the old man's nose?

"Let's go back to last night. You returned to the entrance of 96 Adelaide West about two fifteen. What did you see there?"

"It was awful. My father was on his back on the sidewalk, and another man was crouching over him. I asked what had happened. He said, 'Someone's bumped off Digby Watt.'"

"His exact words?"

"Yes, 'bumped off'."

"And how did you react?"

"I was upset, naturally. I couldn't tell you exactly what I said. I do recall his suggesting one of us call the police. I asked him to do it as I didn't want to leave my father's side."

"Can you describe this man?"

"Tall, thin, with a moustache. Neither dark nor fair. He wore slacks and a windbreaker. He had a rucksack on the ground beside him. He looked like he might have been on his way out of town for a spot of hiking or fishing, but I gather he's a journalist. He gave me this card." Morris took his billfold from an inside jacket pocket and from it extracted Ivan MacAllister's card.

"I don't need that right now," I said after looking it over. "But could you hang on to it, please. What was in this rucksack?"

"I didn't see. Is it important?"

"Did you see a gun anywhere?"

"Definitely not."

"While he was away phoning, were you alone with your father?"

"Yes, the street was quite deserted. There may have been a car drive by, but I couldn't swear to it."

"What did you do during that period?"

"Naturally, I checked first to see if there had been a mistake, to see if my father might still be alive. That is, I checked for a pulse."

"And...?"

"None. It still seems incredible. Gunned down in the streets, as if by rumrunners—and right outside his own office."

"Apart from checking for a pulse, did you touch your father's clothes or body?"

"No."

"I'm sorry to have to raise this subject," I said. And I was sorry. Morris seemed such a gentle soul. "When you first saw your father lying on the sidewalk, was his fly open?"

Morris wiped his nose, and his voice became quieter. "Believe it or not, sergeant, I didn't see. It was only when the other man came back and drew my attention to what had been done...there...that I noticed."

"And what exactly did you notice?"

"That my father's member was outside his trousers. At that point, I took off my topcoat and covered him up with it until the police came and asked me to remove it."

"Ah." I cleared my throat. "Can you think of any explanation for your father's state of undress?"

Morris shook his head miserably.

"Forgive my asking, but might he have been about to relieve himself?"

"Good God, sergeant. I wouldn't want your job on any terms—not if you have to ask questions like that. The last place he would have relieved himself, even in an emergency, would have been against his own front door. He was proud of this building and all the businesses he conducted from here."

I didn't think I could shock him more, so I pressed on. "Was he sexually active?"

"A widower of my father's age?"

"Look here, Mr. Watt, either your father exposed himself or someone interfered with him. I can't ignore that. His condition may tell us something about the motive for the murder. I ask you again: did your father have a sex life at the time of his death?"

"I don't believe so."

"Since he was widowed?"

"I don't know."

"You sound less sure. Have you had any suspicions?"

"Sergeant, I refuse to speculate further, and if you wish this conversation to continue, it will have to be on other topics."

I wondered if he had ever used the words "I refuse" with his father. I helped myself to a couple of mints wrapped in cellophane from a dish on his desk and changed course.

"Let's go back to last night," I said. "When did your cab arrive?"

"I didn't notice the time, but it was just before the constable went to phone the doctor. I asked the driver to wait. I wanted to stay at the scene until a proper medical man had pronounced my father dead. But when the constable got back from phoning, he convinced me that that was already beyond question." Morris made a visible effort to pull himself together and spoke the next words briskly. "I saw I could do nothing more there, so I went home. That must have been shortly before three, say five minutes of."

It struck me that Morris's cab had been a long time coming. He had phoned at 2:09, and the car had pulled up just before 2:45, which was when the constable said he had called for the medical examiner. But then I seemed to remember Platinum was an uptown outfit, handy to the mansions of Rosedale but with no stand in the Bay-Adelaide neighbourhood.

"To your knowledge," I said, moving on, "had your father received any threats?"

"No."

"Can you think of anyone that might have killed him?"

"Absolutely not. He didn't move in that kind of world."

The first hint of snobbery—but more than I could pass over in silence.

"We all live in the same world, Mr. Watt," I said. "Like it or not, your father was gunned down. Who would that have made happy?"

"No one," Morris sighed. "He was a great philanthropist. In the past five years, he gave away more money than he took home."

"Business rivals?" I suggested. "Former partners or employees?"

"His rivals weren't his enemies. They knew his success was due to long hours of hard work, and they respected him for it. And for all the hard work, he always was good-humoured and generous towards the people he worked with. You can ask anyone."

"What about labour disruptions?"

"He treated his workers well. The proof of that is that out of a work force of over eighteen thousand, only one plant felt it necessary to have a union."

"That would be at Canada Ski and Snowshoe," I recalled. "There was a strike there two years ago. Some of the plant machinery was destroyed."

"Communist organizers had turned the workers' heads. In two and a half weeks, the men were back making sporting goods, and new local leadership had been voted in."

"What was the name of the strike leader?"

"It was... No, I'd better not guess, but I'll look it up and send it to you if you think it's important."

"Could be," I said. "Was your father involved with rumrunners in any way?"

"None. That's an absurd question—frankly, uncalled-for."

"You're the one who mentioned rumrunners. Why was that?"

"Just because of the shootouts on the street you hear about. There was one in Alberta not many years ago."

I searched my memory. "The town of Coleman, in 1922, but that was a policeman they killed. His relevance to the liquor trade was obvious. What was your father's? How outspoken was he on the temperance issue?"

"He gave one or two addresses on the subject. Then again, I don't see why that should make him enemies: without prohibitionists, there could be no rumrunners."

"True, sir, but his advocating stricter enforcement of liquor laws could have caused them inconvenience."

"Well, as I believe he realized to his sorrow, my father—for all his business success—didn't have that much influence with the law enforcers."

"Someone must have benefited from Digby Watt's death," I observed. "Was he engaged to be married?"

"To Olive? No. No, he enjoyed spending time with her, but I don't believe he was interested in remarrying."

"If he had married Olive," I asked, nudging the limits, "do you think the marriage would have been consummated?"

"I don't think he would have married Olive Teddington."

"Or anyone else?"

"There was no one else."

"Are you aware of the provisions of your father's will?"

"About that, I suggest you speak to his lawyer." Morris took a card from his desk drawer and wrote from memory. "Here are his particulars."

I didn't press him, as the work day already promised to be long enough. I could get the acting detective to contact the lawyer.

"Anything else I can do for you?"

Morris seemed composed enough to make it safe to return to the subject of the broken-down car. I asked where it could be found at this moment.

"Still on the roof of Braddock's Garage. Curtis offered to come down and repair it this morning, but I said I preferred him to wait until I knew whether you people wanted to look it over. I asked Cliff Braddock to leave it where it was and make sure it wasn't disturbed."

"Exactly right. Could you show me?"

Morris pulled a black-covered agenda towards him across the cherrywood and looked at a page marked by an elastic band.

"Yes," he said. "I can do that."

When we stood, I noticed for the first time a loose wire lying on the surface of the desk and ending where one would have expected Morris's intercom to be. I picked up the unattached wire.

"In for repairs?" I asked.

He nodded. "I just discovered yesterday that when I connect with the reception desk, the switch sometimes sticks in the on position. Don't know how long it's been like that. I hope they fix it soon, though. It's hard on Miss Burgess having always to run in here instead of buzzing."

It was on the tip of my tongue to suggest he move into his father's office, but perhaps it was too soon for so bold a move.

As we passed through the fourth-floor reception area, Morris told the woman with the pince-nez that he would be out of the office for half an hour to an hour.

"Would you advise Mr. Tremblay of Beaconsfield Power I'll see him this afternoon."

"He's catching the noon train back to Montreal, Mr. Morris. It would be better if you saw him now."

"Please ask him to take the four-thirty train instead, Miss Burgess. Perhaps you'd be good enough to phone Union Station and get his ticket changed."

"Mr. Watt would not have asked him to inconvenience himself that way," she said.

"I'm the only Mr. Watt there is at present, Miss Burgess. Thank you."

Morris's jaw was set during the ride down on the elevator; he did not respond to Harold's greeting.

Chapter Three

I timed our walk along busy sidewalks to the garage on Pearl Street at three minutes. Even allowing for an absence of competing traffic after eleven p.m., Morris would have to step lively to make it there on foot and back in the car in five minutes, but—in clear weather, at least—the round trip might not take much longer.

Braddock's Garage was a low white stucco building with a British American Oil Company sign and a couple of pumps out front. A ramp at the right side, overlooked by a window, allowed cars to drive up to and down from the roof. Morris and I walked up.

At this hour, neatly aligned cars filled the rooftop parking area. A few roadsters and touring models in daring shades of maroon, navy or military green surprised the eye, but most of the men who drove or were driven to work downtown plainly favoured the comfort of a closed car and the anonymous dignity of black. One black Gray-Dort sedan looked as if it would have been happy to line up with the rest, but found itself conspicuously jutting into the centre aisle and marked off-limits by a ring of sawhorses. I did a circuit of it with Morris, taking care neither of us touched any knob or surface. This buggy wasn't what you'd call a luxury car, but was certainly closer in size and price to a Cadillac than to a Model T Ford. The choice of a man without false humility but of modest tastes. Furthermore, Digby Watt hadn't required the fad of the moment. Gray-Dort were no longer in business, and the automobile before us wasn't even the last model out the door of their shop—although you could see that the bodywork and upholstery had been kept in tip-top shape.

I had a look underneath. Removing my jacket, I lay on my back and, at much expense to the cleanliness of my white shirt, got under the car. I wriggled to the area where a succession of gears and rods and pin joints were supposed to link the steering column to the left front wheel, which was tied by further rods to the right. The last pin before the left front wheel was not there. For a better look, I struck a match. There was no question about it. The end of the rod with its circular hole was hanging out in space a good four inches from the corresponding hole in the steering arm on the wheel. Under such conditions, the steering wheel would be no more than a toy.

"Mr. Watt," I said, dragging myself out from under the car, "do you ever do repairs on this car yourself?"

"Never, sergeant."

"Does Curtis?"

"Indeed he does, though there may be some heavy work he'd call on a garage for. One thing you can be sure of: if Curtis does any work, it's well done."

I pulled on my jacket, making a mental note not to take it off again until I had a chance to change my shirt.

Meanwhile, a balding, yellow-haired man in his fifties sauntered up the ramp, hands on his thick hips. He wore a clean pair of green jodhpurs and a matching waist-belted jacket on the breast pocket of which "Clifford Braddock" was stitched in red thread. Through the vee of the jacket peeked a white shirt and shiny black bow-tie. His head resembled a watermelon in shape and size, while his well-fed face expressed a sixty-forty blend of curiosity and concern. Morris introduced me to the garage owner.

"Terrible news about Mr. Watt. Dreadful. A man of real substance. Do you have any idea, detective, of who could have done it?" Braddock's forehead crumpled into deep lines. His voice was grave but mellifluous—and he clearly liked the sound of it, for he said the same thing two or three more times in different words.

"Do *you* know of anyone that might have wanted him dead, sir?" I asked.

Braddock said he could think of no one and said so in a variety of ways. Apparently all business with the garage had been conducted by Morris. Braddock had not known Digby Watt to speak to, only by sight. I had little more to ask the garage owner, apart from confirming what Morris had said about the security of the parked cars at night. Whatever value a chain might have in preventing theft, it plainly did nothing to keep out saboteurs.

"I've tried hiring night watchmen," Braddock sighed, "but they always fall asleep on the job, and then how are my customers further ahead? I mean to say—I keep an eye on who comes up here any time before seven or eight at night. I noticed you gentlemen this morning right enough. But there's a limit to what I can do after I've gone home. That is, what's the point of paying someone—"

"Did you," I interrupted, "or any of your people, see anyone tampering with the Watt car yesterday?"

A string of denials. Braddock claimed to have quizzed his staff up and down on the subject.

"I'm going to have this vehicle towed," I said. "Please leave it where it is till then."

"Certainly, sir. Right you are. Very good. Taking it to headquarters, are you?"

Of course, I thought, park it on Sanderson's desk.

"The garage at Station Number One will do nicely," I told him. "We're a square foot or two short of space at City Hall. One more thing, Mr. Braddock. As you'll see if you stick your head under here, there's a pin missing from the steering gear. You'll be able to give the piece its proper name. I'll be instructing the police mechanic who comes for the car to look around the roof for that little pin. If you or any of your men find it in the meantime, I'd like it picked up with pliers and put in an envelope."

"Can you take fingerprints off something that fiddly?" asked Morris, who had been quiet and seemingly incurious about the Gray-Dort's problems.

"I don't know," I said, "but I'm not taking any chances."

"No indeed, sir," Braddock chimed in. "Of course not. Last thing you should do."

We left the garage owner on his roof.

"Thank you for your time this morning, Mr. Watt," I said as we made our way down the ramp. I was busting a gut not to let my irritation show. It irked me that a man of the consequence of Digby Watt hadn't made better provision for his car, hadn't kept a closer eye on important machinery. "Too bad about that missed appointment."

"The appointment is postponed, not missed, sergeant, and with more than sufficient reason. We all hope you solve this murder on the double."

The military expression prompted me to ask which outfit he'd served with.

"Oh, I did clerical work at a supply depot in Guildford," he replied. "Never got across the Channel, I'm afraid."

"Do any small arms training?"

"No, I was just a lance corporal. We didn't have pistols."

"Are you in possession of any firearms now?"

"I suppose you have to ask that. My father has a rifle at

his summer cottage on Lake Simcoe. No one in the family has any pistols. Not as far as I know."

I tried to imagine the sort of old rifle that would be left lying around a cottage, used at most for potting away at groundhogs. Likely the wrong calibre—all but certainly incapable of firing fast enough to group that trio of holes in its owner's waistcoat. Might as well be thorough, however.

"What rifle is it, Mr. Watt?"

"Something Remington presented him with in his capacity as president of Canada Ski and Snowshoe. A Model Something Autoloader."

"Model 8 Autoloading," I said. A rapid-fire weapon after all. "There are variants chambered for four different cartridge sizes. Which one did they give him?"

"There you have me, sergeant. I might find the letter from the manufacturer in the files. Or, if you're going over to the house, my sister may be able to tell you."

Chapter Four

Through the front window of the approaching Bay Street tram, I recognized the driver's mug, so I stuck my head around the partition into the cockpit once I'd hauled myself aboard.

"Tricky steering here, Captain," I cautioned as the wide double-truck car jogged north through the Queen Street intersection past a similar tub jogging south. The TTC had actually had to dig up the tracks on all the major routes and move them farther apart to permit these new streetcars to pass each other. "Watch you don't scrape his paint."

"You again!" The driver managed simultaneously to shoot me a look of mock disgust and ring his bell at a pedestrian apparently bent on becoming Toronto's tenth traffic fatality of the year. "How long do you have to work at that cop shop of yours before they let you have a car?"

"Ah, Fred, I've no place to keep a car."

It was a good question, though, and I continued trying to answer it once I'd moved back to give the conductor my fare and fold myself into an empty space on one of the longitudinal, wood-slat benches. Not only was the department not making an automobile available, but they steadfastly refused to reimburse detectives for cab fare. So after I'd finished bouncing up Bay Street, I could look forward to a transfer onto the Bloor car eastbound as far as Sherbourne Street and a long walk north. Possibly a wet one, as afternoon had brought back the clouds. This was no style in which to investigate the murder of a bigwig.

Then inspiration struck. I ignored the stop at Bloor and continued up Bay to Davenport, where I dropped in at the city's mounted police unit. I wasn't about to trade my kingdom for a horse, but I'd heard that some well-ridden motorcycles headed for the junk yard were temporarily stored in the back of the stables. With the help of a bored groom, I picked out the most roadworthy, stirred it into sputtering life and set it hurtling down Rosedale Valley Road with me on its back.

It's not hard to get lost in Rosedale, but there is one straight street—the one where the Watts lived. This mazelike luxury suburb with its ravine lots was dreamed up in the nineteenth century, but not developed till the twentieth when cars made it get-at-able and, just as important, when the elite no longer had the unlimited Victorian appetite for parading their wealth. They could no longer be as sure as their forefathers that folks would respect riches as a sign of divine favour—rather than resent them as evidence of social injustice. So while you might want it known you lived somewhere in Rosedale, that didn't necessarily mean you wanted your house easily found.

In this regard as in others, Digby Watt had seemed to straddle the centuries—not enough of an exhibitionist to live downtown on Queen's Park Crescent, but far from a shrinking violet.

His palatial house on Glen Road had a curving drive and a porte-cochère. I parked the decrepit Harley-Davidson smack in front of the front door to show I wasn't intimidated by the place, but I did comb my hair and pop a peppermint in my mouth to camouflage the smell of the beer I'd had for lunch—all of which was just as well, because the freckled housemaid who answered my knock was kitted out in a fresh grey uniform whose pressed creases would have put a guards regiment to shame.

Despite her business-as-usual smartness, there was no hiding that her eyes were red from crying. I got her to say that her name was Nita and that she had been in service with the Watts for four years, since she was sixteen.

The ladies of the household were drinking tea in the conservatory overlooking the back garden. I'd spoken by telephone to Mrs. Morris Watt, who was expecting me, but it seemed Morris's sister Edith had just come home and didn't know me from Adam. I overheard the words "man who'll solve the mystery" pass in earnest undertones between the two even as Nita was showing me a path through the palms and aspidistras. In more ways than one, the heat was on.

Mrs. Watt wore a modestly cut, expensive dress of a navy blue that went well with her permanently waved blonde hair. She rose to greet me promptly and yet with a sort of indolence I took as typically modern and by no means a personal slight. In fact, her social manner was faultless, considerate without seeming too hostessy, appropriate to so serious an occasion as the death of a father-in-law. I tried to picture her with Morris. Her husband would see in her someone brought up with standards of behaviour similar to his own, and with that extra polish women were expected to have. He would appreciate also her womanly figure, and value perhaps a confidence lacking in himself. If Morris were sexually shy, I had the feeling she wouldn't be. Where did such an impression come from? My experience of women didn't extend to this level of society, but I thought I recognized what Mrs. Watt possessed. Of the couple, Morris had more in the way of movie star looks. His consort's complexion was rough, rougher than her face powder could completely smooth over; there were too many teeth in her mouth; her grey-green eyes didn't point quite in the same direction; and her hips were already starting to spread. Nonetheless, a man who felt desired by her might well think her beautiful. Morris might.

"I got the death notice in all the papers, Lavinia," her sister-in-law rattled on breathlessly, "but there's trouble brewing at City Hall. They want some kind of state funeral, which I can't bear the thought of."

"Edith," said Mrs. Watt, "this is Detective Sergeant Paul Shenstone, the policeman who's investigating the case."

"One of them," I grinned. I liked "investigate" better than "solve". Nice of her to lower expectations when speaking aloud.

"Oh, yes. Hello. Nita, take my coat, would you?"

Housemaid and coat melted silently away.

Edith Watt wore a black, pleated skirt and white blouse that accentuated her schoolgirl freshness. She was past school age, but young enough. Too young to have been prepared for anything like what had happened in the past few hours. Still, she was pitching in with family duties, not leaving them to those with more the hang of death and funerals. Flustered, yes, but not necessarily weak. Maybe she just didn't think she had to put on a show of composure in front of family and servants. Public servants included.

She had all her brother's good looks and more. Very dark, glossy hair with a part just off centre, down-sloping eyes of the most vivid blue, an upper lip that dipped in the middle and swelled softly to either side to form naturally that Cupid's bow so prized at present and so badly approximated with cosmetics. A grin-and-bear-it style of grief wouldn't have suited her at all.

"I'm sorry to have to disturb you today," I said.

"I'm not sure anything could make this day any worse," Edith sighed.

"And the sooner you get to work, the better the chance of finding our father's killer, I'm sure," said Lavinia. "Sit, Mr. Shenstone, and tell me how you take your tea."

"I'll bet he takes it clear."

"Correct, Miss Watt." I took the cup, a chair, and careful note of the tear-dewed blue eyes fixed upon me. "Can you each tell me when you first heard of your father's death?"

Lavinia began. I dragged my attention her way.

"My husband woke me when he came in. It was three or a little after. 'You've never been this late,' I said. And he said, 'Father's been murdered.' "

"Go on."

"This *is* difficult." Lavinia smiled bravely. "We were all so fond of Father. Well, when Morris came in, I was pretty groggy and I asked him if this was a nightmare he was telling me about. He said no, that Father had been shot down in the street outside his office. The idea was horrifying, but I still don't think I was quite taking it in. 'Who by?' I think I asked, and he said, that would be for the police to find out. And here you are." Lavinia paused. "And then he asked if I would wake Edith, and I said to let her sleep, that she'd need to be well-rested for all she'd have to go through today—yes, Edie, I know that was very wrong of me..."

"Very," said Edith sternly.

"But then Morris went and told you, so *that* was all right anyway."

"Miss Watt?" I said.

"I was awakened by knocking on my door. I sprang up with a premonition of something dreadful and reached for my robe. I turned on the light on the bedside table. I said,

'Come in,' and Morris came in. He said, 'I'm afraid I have hard news, sis. Dad's been murdered.' I asked if he was sure, and he said yes. 'Here, in his sleep?' I asked, and Morris said no, in front of the office, while he was coming home."

"Why did you ask if your father had been murdered in this house?" I said.

"Just because it was the middle of the night."

"Before your brother, who was the last person you saw last night?"

"Lavinia—Mrs. Watt. She was going to bed, and I said I'd sit up downstairs and read for a while."

"What time was that?"

"Jeepers, I don't know."

"Perhaps I can answer Mr. Shenstone. The hall clock had just struck eleven."

"Thank you, Mrs. Watt. And you were both asleep when Morris Watt came into the house?"

"Yes."

"Yes."

"Neither of you heard his taxi pull up?"

"No."

"No."

"Does the family have a second car?"

"An Austin Chummy," said Edith. "I was just downtown in it."

"And was that car out last night?"

Both women said not.

"Would it," I asked, "have been possible to take the Chummy out without your knowledge—after you were both asleep? Neither of you heard Morris's taxi, remember."

"That's true," said Lavinia. "The Chummy *is* pretty rackety. Sounds like a motorcycle. I can't imagine anyone would drive it around in the middle of the night, but I sleep soundly as a rule. I might not have heard it."

"I certainly would have," Edith leaped in. "I sleep lightly, and my bedroom is in the back of the house, at the end towards the garage. No one could have taken a car out without my hearing, and last night no one did."

"Did either of you leave the house between the time you parted and the time Mr. Morris Watt returned?"

"No," twice.

"And neither of you saw anyone else during that period?"

"No," said Edith.

"Actually, I did," Lavinia confessed. "I rang for Nita when I got to bed and had her bring me a cup of cocoa. It would have been about eleven thirty when she brought the cocoa and left."

"The cocoa was part of your regular bedtime routine?"

"Father didn't like keeping the servants up that late. So I only did it if he wasn't home by the time I went to bed. I suppose you'll think I'm awful going behind his back like that, but I truly didn't mean any disrespect. And of course I wouldn't have done it if I had known... Oh, excuse me."

While Lavinia was sobbing into her handkerchief, Edith jumped in.

"He knew you loved him, Vinnie. One just thinks of the strangest things at a time like this. Like the way I laughed at Dad for stringing up a new radio antenna every two weeks. He acted as though with just enough wire stretched in just the right shape, he would be able to receive the one elusive broadcast that would transform his life. And now he's gone, I don't feel like laughing one bit, and I really wish he had been able to listen to what he was looking for with all those festoons of wire."

Here was a new side of the deceased. I put aside my tea

and leaned forward with my elbows on my knees.

"Did Digby Watt want his life transformed? From outside, it would seem he had done pretty well."

"I think..." Lavinia pulled herself together, "I think everyone, however successful, wants something they haven't got. Greener grass and all that."

"Let's talk about your late father-in-law, though," I insisted. "Couldn't he have bought the greenest grass there is? Or even have hired a lab full of scientists to invent something greener?"

"I don't know if Edith agrees, but to me he seemed bored. I mean, he never gave me the idea—or Morris, for that matter—that there was anything he was looking forward to doing. Certainly not retiring. I mean, he believed in an afterlife and everything, but in the meantime, while you're still here, you still have the days and nights to get through."

"Daddy wasn't bored," said Edith. "He was still building and improving his businesses. And—what maybe mattered more to him at this stage—he had his charitable work. I thought he was sad, though. As you know, my mother died two years ago, and that was a cruel blow, but it was more than that."

"What more?" I asked, getting in just ahead of Lavinia.

"It's so difficult to say. We sometimes know things without knowing how we know them. Something to do with his faith, perhaps. We're all churchgoers, but he was the only one of us that really had faith."

"Morris is a Christian," said Lavinia. "It's very sweet of him."

Edith seemed not to hear her. "I recall some snatch of a sermon or prayer that seemed to hit Dad hard. I think it was just before this Easter. The minister said, 'Too often we nurse the pain others cause us while blotting from our minds the pain we cause.'"

"I hate pain," said Lavinia. "I don't even like to think about it."

"The minister reminded him of someone he'd hurt?" I asked.

"I couldn't tell," said Edith. "He was a typical businessman who kept work and home separate. He didn't want us to worry about what went on at the office. That didn't mean he had guilty secrets; it was just his generation's way." She folded her napkin thoughtfully. "I do know he'd recently started carrying around a little book of inspirational quotations. Now we learn that very book saved him from one of the bullets. Strange, isn't it? I had a look at it on the weekend. Its message for most days seems to be patience in adversity."

"Do either of you know if he had received any threats?"

Both women said no.

"Did either of you ever hear him argue or have an angry scene with anyone?"

Again the fair and dark heads shook as one.

"He believed in the duty of cheerfulness," Edith added. "He was never even bad-humoured that I recall."

"Nor I."

"Anyone bad-humoured with *him?*"

"Mrs. Hubbard—" Lavinia began.

"That's our cook," Edith explained.

"—scolds him unmercifully about missing meals, but she dotes on him."

"No one else?"

"No."

"This must be maddening for you, Mr. Shenstone," said Lavinia, "but we just can't think of anyone wishing Father ill. It seems inconceivable."

"What about Curtis?"

"Curtis? I wouldn't say Curtis doted on him, would you, Vinnie?"

"How would one know? Curtis is quiet." Lavinia dropped her voice to a whisper. "Quiet as a mummy."

"Works well, though."

"Very."

I wrote in my notebook. "So at present the household consists of yourselves, Mr. Morris Watt, Mrs. Hubbard, Nita, and Curtis?"

"That's right," said Lavinia.

"Curtis lives over the garage," Edith added, "not in the house proper."

"Are there any firearms about the property at all, in the house or the garage?"

"Oh, no," said Lavinia.

"Not that I know of," said Edith.

"Can either of you think of anyone, inside the house or out, who might have killed your father?"

I braced myself for another chorus of "No, not a soul!" But neither woman spoke. Each stole a glance at the other.

"Would you prefer to interview us separately?" Lavinia asked me.

"Not for the present."

"I certainly have nothing to say I wouldn't want Edith to hear. I can't think of anyone."

"Neither can I, not off the top of my head. Mr. Shenstone, do you know what my father did in the war?"

I shifted in my chair.

"It's hot in here, isn't it, Mr. Shenstone?" said Lavinia. "Do take off your jacket. We're not as formal as you may think."

I hadn't yet changed my shirt and left my jacket on. What I was really itching to do was tell them what I knew rather than find out what they did. Tell them why I hadn't shed any tears yet for Digby Watt and wasn't about to start.

"What *did* your father do, Miss Watt?"

"I've only the vaguest idea. He was too old to enlist, of course, so he continued to run his businesses, tailoring them to the demands of the war effort."

"And do you believe that had anything to do with his murder?"

"How would I know? I was only ten in 1914. It's just that he sometimes spoke of the years before the war with such nostalgia. No, I can't be more precise: don't ask me."

"All right." I turned to Lavinia. "Mrs. Watt, did he ever speak to you about the war or the years before?"

"Not about his factories or anything like that. But right before our marriage, he did say I had him to thank for Morris's coming back in one piece. Morris had wanted to get into the fighting, but Father had used his contacts to make sure his requests for a transfer were turned down. I think he didn't want my thanks so much as he wanted me to know it was no reflection on Morris's courage that he didn't see action in France."

"I had no idea!" Edith exclaimed. "I kept writing him in England, asking when he was going to get into the scrap. How cruel! But I think the girls, even children, were as war-drunk as the men."

Silence settled on the conservatory, and for the first time I noticed the murmur of the house—a humming pipe, the tap of the housemaid's shoes crossing a hardwood floor, the distant clink of dishes being taken out or put away—and further in the background, the purr of traffic from Glen Road. Had Morris and Lavinia ever considered moving out of these comfy precincts into a space of their own?

I was also asking myself whether Digby's words to Lavinia

had done Morris's character any good, or had been intended to. Before, she might have just thought her husband averse to getting killed. Culpably or commendably prudent, but his own man. After, she must realize that whatever Morris's willingness to serve as Imperial cannon fodder, he hadn't had the gumption to get out from under Daddy's thumb and join an outfit beyond the reach of Daddy's pull. Would the Italians have cared a fig for the wishes of Digby Watt? The Serbians? The Arabs? There were more than enough belligerents to choose from. What Digby had been telling Lavinia, it seemed to me, was that as long as Digby was alive, Digby's was the word that counted in the Watt family, and Morris would be kept on leading strings.

"How did that news make you feel, Mrs. Watt?" I said at last.

"I thought," she replied, "how sweet of Father. He looks after us all."

"I see. What are the provisions of his will?"

"Here's what he told me," Edith jumped in, as if grateful to get rolling again. "A pension for Mrs. Hubbard. Lump sum bequests for Nita and Curtis. I was to get a life annuity with the principal to be divided among my children, if any. I don't know what provision he made for Lavinia and Morris, but I'd be surprised if he hadn't left generous contributions to the various hospitals and servicemen's associations he supported."

"You know much more than I do, Edie," said Lavinia, her social manner clearly in a struggle with hurt feelings. "Neither Father nor Morris said anything to me."

"Never mind," said Edith, still brisk and with a new hardness in her voice. "It would all have had to change anyway when Dad remarried."

"Did you expect him to?" I asked.

"Yes," said Edith.

"Marry Olive?" said Lavinia. "I don't think he would have. She's a darling girl, but she's *your* age, Edie."

"There's no law that makes that wrong, and I don't think he saw it as wrong."

"She's young for her age, though." Lavinia crossed her legs and touched her hair, less to tidy it than to draw attention to its golden perfection. "She leads a very sheltered life, living with her aunt, selling flowers in her aunt's flower shop. Olive herself must know she hasn't the poise to carry off marriage to a more seasoned man."

"She'd be the person to ask what she knows," Edith replied as from a high and frosty peak.

Lavinia laughed complacently. Olive had been no thorn in *her* side, I thought, but sure got under missy's skin.

"And you, Miss Watt? Did you see it as wrong?"

"Wrong, no. It just made me queasy, because I'd imagine myself in Olive's place. But I wasn't in Olive's place. My father had never treated me as anything but a daughter. As I was saying, I thought Dad was unhappy, and the best part of me wanted for him anything that would make him less so, even if that thing were a twenty-two-year-old wife."

While they were good words, prettily arranged, Edith's expression remained a degree below freezing, and I guessed her heart did too.

I wrote down Olive's address. I might, I warned, have more questions later. Meanwhile, I'd like to take a look around the garage and have a word with Curtis.

"I'll show him through, Edie," said Lavinia.

"Mr. Shenstone," said Edith, "I look forward to seeing you again."

"Likewise, Miss Watt."

"You know," Edith continued with new animation, "I've

been thinking this over while we've been talking, and it seems to me that that minister left out one kind of pain. Besides the pain others cause us and the pain we cause, there's the pain others cause our loved ones, and cause our neighbours—you know, neighbours in the fullest biblical sense. That pain isn't ours, and we have no right to blot it out. What that pain requires is justice."

I could have kissed her for that. Instead, I nodded offhandedly and followed Lavinia from the room.

Chapter Five

Lavinia led me through a long dining room to a set of French doors. From here, above a tall cedar hedge that formed the left border of the rose garden, I could see the peaked roof of the garage. Before letting me out, however, Lavinia touched my arm confidentially.

"I didn't want to say anything in front of Edith, Mr. Shenstone, but there's one question I would like to ask you."

I nodded.

"Is there any chance that my father-in-law took his own life?"

"Did he say or do anything that makes you think he meant to?"

At my counter-question, Lavinia clapped a hand to her breast—as if she feared the shock might endanger her heart. Her eyes got round.

"Oh no!"

"You said you thought your father-in-law was bored. Bored enough not to want to live?"

"It sounds ridiculous. It is ridiculous. Preposterous. But maybe no *more* preposterous than the idea that someone else mightn't have wanted him to live. Do you see, Mr. Shenstone? I was just wondering if the physical circumstances of the shooting allowed for—for the possibility of..." Her voice trailed off.

"What did your husband tell you about the gun?"

"That none was found, and that's what the paper says too. But still—a passerby might have picked it up."

"You'd need a nimble trigger finger, Mrs. Watt, to fire a pair of bullets into the same part of your own chest, even if a third one strayed into *Daily Strength for Daily Needs*."

"I see," said Lavinia. "Thank you." She held half of one of the double doors open for me.

I hesitated.

"How long have you and Mr. Watt been married?"

"Three years this June. Why do you ask?"

"I was just wondering how well you knew Digby Watt."

"I wonder too. But I knew him before my marriage. I'm from Winnipeg, you know, and he used to come out on business. He was setting up a packing house there with my father. Dad insisted Mr. Watt have a home-cooked dinner with the family at least once each visit. One evening, he told me that next time he came west, he'd bring his son Morris. And he did." A lift and drop to her shoulders let it be understood that there was nothing more to say, that it had been love at first sight on both sides.

All the same, if Digby had been a widower at the time of those trips to Winnipeg, I'm not sure Morris would have had a chance.

"If your father-in-law had remarried," I said, "do you think he might have had more children?"

"Sure." Mrs. Watt gave me a knowing look. "Why not?"

I grinned in acknowledgement and stepped out into the garden. I had to turn sideways to get through the narrow opening without brushing against her.

When I rounded the hedge, I found a compact man of soldierly bearing washing a blue Austin, presumably the car he had taken Edith downtown in this morning, since the Gray-Dort was unavailable. Or perhaps she had driven herself. With its sky-bright colour, its black cloth roof that could be thrown away in good weather, and a wheelbase scarcely more than six feet, it looked to my eyes thoroughly girlish.

"Help you?" The voice was deep, the tone reproving.

"Would you be Curtis?"

"Yes."

"I'm Detective Sergeant Shenstone, here to investigate Mr. Watt's murder. Could I have your first name?"

"Curtis. It's Curtis Ritter." After taking a good look at my wallet badge, the chauffeur put his sponge in the bucket and set it down on the cement apron before the detached garage. He dried his hands on a cloth hung over his shoulder. His face beneath short, sandy hair was square and grave. "I prefer," he said, "to be called Curtis."

I noticed that his grey uniform jodhpurs seemed new.

"How long have you been working for the Watts?"

"Since Thanksgiving."

"And before that?"

"I was in Ottawa."

"In Parliament?"

I was hoping Curtis's stiff features might soften up a bit. Even a lame crack has been known to get a smile. Not this time.

"In jail. Mr. Watt knew."

"What were you there for?"

"Carriage of liquor. In from Quebec."

I pictured to myself the advantages of police work in the national capital. The prospect of living on the Ottawa River, a mere bridge-length away from a wet province, made my throat tickle.

"Mainly," Curtis added, "I kept the smugglers' cars running."

"Running faster than the cops', I bet."

Curtis stuck out his lower lip.

"What can you tell me about Mr. Watt's murder?"

"Nothing. I didn't drive him yesterday."

"When did you hear about his death?"

"This morning at breakfast."

"Were you surprised?"

"Certainly."

"Do you have any firearms?"

"No. And don't think I used any while I was mixed up with the rumrunners. My work began and ended with the cars."

"You don't know of any enemies Digby Watt might have had?"

"None."

"What was your own impression of him?"

"He gave me work, even though I had a record. I thought highly of him."

"You didn't drive him yesterday. What did you do?"

"I took Mrs. Morris Watt shopping in the afternoon, and when she said she wouldn't be needing me again, I went out."

"In this car?"

"Shank's mare."

"Where did you walk to?"

"There's a garage on Bloor Street East—Stone's. I work there when I'm sure not to be needed here."

"Mr. Watt didn't pay well?"

"He paid well, but I wanted to build up some savings."

"What are you saving for, Curtis?"

"A rainy day."

"A business of your own perhaps."

"Perhaps."

"Marriage?"

Again Curtis's lip went out in that deprecatory pout. "That depends on her."

"Who?"

"I don't care to say."

"Do you think she'd be keener to marry you if you had more money?"

"No, that's not the way she thinks."

"What time did you get back here last night?"

"Eleven thirty or so."

"Did you see anyone when you returned?"

"The light was on in the kitchen, so I went in to see who was up. Nita was making cocoa for Mrs. Morris. I gave her a hand, and when she went upstairs I came out to bed. Close to midnight."

"You gave Nita a hand," I said. "And no one saw you again till morning?"

"No."

"Could you have left your room without anyone's hearing? I'm speaking of anyone in the house."

"Certainly I could have. But I didn't."

"And you could have taken this Austin Chummy out with no one the wiser. The engine is loud, but the car's small enough that you could have wheeled it out to the street before starting it."

"I've never—"

"Curtis, did your employer tell you there was a bequest for you in his will?"

"Once in jail, always a suspect, eh? It's nonsense, though. As I say, I'd worked for him only half a year. Why would he leave me money?"

"Perhaps," I hazarded, "because he enjoyed your warm, outgoing personality and your inexhaustible fund of amusing chatter. Look, friend, I don't know why he would leave you money, but did he or anyone else ever suggest to you he was doing so?"

"No, no one did."

The garage was a double one, deep and high ceilinged. Through the open doors, I could make out a workbench running along the back wall in the space under the steep stairs up to Curtis's quarters.

"Are there just the two cars?"

"Yes."

"I'm told you do a good job of keeping them running. Let's have a look at your tools."

Curtis turned on a couple of bright electric lights in the work area. The surface of the wooden bench was scrubbed and, but for a metal tool-box, perfectly clear. Spare wheels and fuel cans were stowed beneath. A set of wrenches hung in order of size on the wall. One shelf held quart cans of lubricant and anti-freeze, another boxes of small spare parts. These latter were labelled for the Austin or the Gray-Dort. I took down one of the latter, then a second. Here Curtis had not sorted quite so fanatically, but I poked about and presently there rested on my open palm a pin that looked as if it might have been at home in a steering linkage.

"What's this?" I asked.

"A steering pin," said Curtis without expression.

"Did you remove it from the Watts' Gray-Dort sedan in the past thirty-six hours?"

"No."

I waited for him to deny ever having seen it before.

"It's a spare," he added.

I held it to the light.

"It looks worn. Not worn out, but used."

"I got it from the garage where I work, from a car that was going to the wreckers."

"Can anyone at Stone's confirm that?"

"That there was a Gray-Dort going to the wreckers, yes. That I took that particular part, no. But—" A breath of feeling ruffled the surface of Curtis's stolid calm. "But if I'd taken this from Mr. Watt's car yesterday, I would not have been so very, very *stupid* as to have kept it for the police to find so easily today."

"Perhaps not," I soothed, wiping a drop of sputtered saliva from my chin. Before the end, I might need to exploit that chink in the chauffeur's self-control, but it was still early in the game. "Tell me, Curtis, could a piece like this come out by accident?"

"It could break," Curtis grunted, "if the metal were faulty."

Chapter Six

I spoke to the remaining staff in the kitchen before leaving Glen Road. They were drinking their tea from mugs, which kept it hotter than the conservatory china. I tried with great gulps to burn out my whisky thirst. I quickly established that the two women's full names were Anita O'Sullivan and Ada Hubbard. The latter had been widowed early in life and had worked for the Watts for more than thirty years.

She corresponded very much to the image I'd formed of the fond, irascible family cook on the verge of pensionability. A pair of bifocals in heavy black frames sat before her bulging brown eyes. She was fleshy without being flabby, and of the hairs that escaped her cap, the grey outnumbered the brown by not less than four to one. The smell of baking pastry was in the air, and steam was rising from a soup pot on the range. I imagined that dinner guests, while they would not be begging for her recipes, would go home neither hungry nor discontented.

"I can see you're in the middle of preparing dinner," I said. "I won't keep you long."

"I don't know who'll have any stomach for it tonight. I've no appetite myself." So saying, Mrs. Hubbard took a comprehensive bite out of a piece of jam-covered bread.

"Why did they shoot him, sir?" asked Nita, pushing her tea aside. "No one could have wanted him dead. It's so awful when the best people are shot, the very best. I thought that ended with the war."

"I say it was a mistake," put in Mrs. Hubbard. "As you say, there's not a person on this earth that could have wanted to harm that sweet man. One gangster probably meant to kill another gangster. People make mistakes all the time, misplace things. Well, if you misplace a bullet, somebody dies. I say get rid of the guns—or at least put them out of reach of the crooks."

"Do you think it was a mistake, sir?" Nita persisted.

I resisted the urge to tell her that shooting someone usually is.

"You'll have heard," I said, "that there's a problem with the car. If it was tampered with, it's hard to see how the shooting can have been an accident or a case of mistaken identity."

"Cars have breakdowns," Mrs. Hubbard countered testily.

"I see what he means, though. Curtis kept the car in tip-top shape."

"I know you won't hear a word against Curtis, Nita dear. All I'm saying is: accidents do happen."

"Nita," I said, "are you and Curtis courting?"

Nita shook her head, but a blush covered her face from her pointed chin to the fringe of her bob. Even her freckles turned red.

"'Course she is," said Mrs. Hubbard, conveying the last bread crumbs from plate to mouth with moistened finger tips. "A most scandalous case of flirting on the job."

"Are you planning to get married?"

"We wanted to, sir, but..."

"I presume the obstacle was lack of money," I said.

"No, not that," Nita replied. "It's my parents. They don't know Curtis like I do, and I can't think of marrying without their blessing. Mr. Watt—Mr. Digby Watt—was going to speak to them and make it all right, but now... Oh, sir, I am sorry for him and for his family, truly, but his dying has just wrecked my chance for happiness utterly."

The tears came faster than she could wipe them, so she did the only thing she could and ran from the room.

"She didn't want to tell you, sir, but the real trouble with her parents is that Curtis has been in the Penitentiary. Not—I want you to know—for anything that could make any sensible person lose any sleep or not want to give him a chance, but—"

"Excuse me, Mrs. Hubbard. Was it the Penitentiary Curtis was in or the Carleton County Jail in Ottawa?"

"Oh, aren't they the same? It was just for three months, in any case."

"That won't have been the Pen. It's down in Kingston, and they don't take a man in there for less than two years."

"No, bless you, nothing like that! I'm sure Nita's mother and father would have listened to Mr. Digby, a man of such upright character, but it'll be hard to find anyone to fill his shoes there any more than in his business world."

"Did Curtis know that Digby Watt was going to speak to Nita's parents on his behalf?"

"I suppose so, but I can't say I ever heard them talk about it. Curtis isn't much of a talker in any case."

"He's certainly wasted no time in gaining the family's trust," I observed. "Morris Watt speaks highly of him."

"That's always been the family way with staff, unless they find reason not to trust."

"And have they ever found reason?"

The cook thoughtfully pushed her bifocals up the bridge of her broad nose.

"Not that I can recall," she said at last.

"Mrs. Hubbard, what became of Curtis's predecessor?" I licked my chops at the prospect of a vengeful ex-employee. "Did he fail to give satisfaction?"

"Lordy, no. Webster was looking for a business opportunity, and Mr. Watt gave him one of the Atkinson stores to manage."

"Atkinson?" I hadn't heard that name before. "Could it have been Atkins hardware?"

"That's what I said. You've never seen a happier man."

The former chauffeur's full name and forwarding address went into my notebook, though I had to admit he didn't sound like a wellspring of bile and rage.

I didn't think there was more work for me here at present, and I still had Olive Teddington to see, but before rising from the kitchen table I trotted out my last stock question.

"You mentioned guns, Mrs. Hubbard. Are there any firearms at all here on the premises?"

"Luckily, none that I know of." She got up to put away the tea things. "None but the rifle from the cottage."

That's what I heard, but I thought I must have forgotten to clean my ears.

"From the cottage on Lake Simcoe? It's here in the city?"

"Oh, yes. Last Thanksgiving when we were closing up, I just wasn't easy in my mind about leaving it there all winter. You know how it is. Every winter one or two cottages get broken into. I hated to have anything to do with it, but I just thought I'll take it to the city for the winter and take it back in the spring. That way it won't fall into the wrong hands. It's the same shape as the vacuum cleaner, I thought, so I'll just pack them together."

"Did you tell anyone you were doing this?"

"I don't remember. Yes, I do: I told Miss Edith."

"And where in the house is the gun stored?"

"Why, I just locked it in the silver closet with the best plate and all the inscribed hardware they presented to Mr. Digby in recognition of his public service. You know, all the hardware he thanked them for but didn't want to have to look at. That's the place."

"Could you show me please, Mrs. Hubbard?"

"Why would you want me to show it to you? That gun had nothing to do with his getting shot."

"Nonetheless."

"You policemen do have peculiar ideas. I'd have to get my keys first."

"Who besides yourself has a key to that closet?"

"No one. Mr. Digby said he had enough other keys to cart around, so I kept them both. Where are they now? Yes, in my room."

I was as interested to see how the keys were stored as how the gun itself was, so I accompanied the cook to the second floor. Access was by a back staircase, but Mrs. Hubbard's quarters were on the same corridor as the principal bedrooms of the house. She did not keep her own door locked, and I could see that it would be easy for anyone to enter her room without her knowledge while she was in the kitchen. Mrs. Hubbard led me through a snug sitting room into a compact bedroom, also unlocked. Beside the large bed in the corner stood a bedside table of green painted wood. She opened the drawer in this table and took from it a ring of half a dozen keys of various sizes. Picking one of the smaller ones to hold the collection by, she led the way back down to the kitchen and from there to the basement. To this level also, I noticed, there were both a back and a front staircase. Beyond the foot of the latter, the cook turned into a storage room of many cupboards, none of which had built-in locks and only one of which was secured by a padlock. This she opened. She proceeded to remove velvet bags whose contents could be surmised by shape to be the inscribed teapots and salvers she had alluded to. I could imagine: *To Acknowledge Digby Watt's Service to the Empire in the Great War, In Grateful Recognition of Digby Watt's Tireless Work on Behalf of the Hospital for Sick Children, To a True Friend of the Rotarians...the Y.M.C.A...the W.C.T.U...the I.O.D.E.* Et cetera. And behind this useless hardware...

"It's gone!" Mrs. Hubbard exclaimed.

"You're sure?"

I helped her make quite sure the rifle was nowhere in that cupboard. When my matches ran out, she fetched a flashlight to supplement the dim bulb hanging from the storeroom ceiling. We checked some other cupboards as well, but the cook was adamant that she would not have stored the gun anywhere without a lock.

"Mrs. Hubbard," I said at last, "let's go find Miss Watt."

"All those stairs," Mrs. Hubbard grumbled. "Still, you can't argue with the police. I'll send her down to you, shall I?"

"No, I'll keep you company." I didn't want there to be any possibility of the inspector's saying Edith and her cook had worked out a story between them.

In the event, we didn't have to return to the second storey. A murmur of voices led us to a ground-floor study. There, on the ingle-bench, Miss Watt sat with her arm around Nita O'Sullivan's drooping shoulders. Edith glared at me as I entered. If it had been the housemaid I had had to lay siege to at that moment, I thought, there'd have been blood on the Axminster carpets.

"Excuse me, Miss Watt. Does your family own a rifle?"

"Yes. It's at the cottage at Roches Point. In the cupboard of my father's bedroom."

"It wasn't brought to the city last fall?"

"No, we never bring it to the city."

"Now, Miss Edith!" Mrs. Hubbard was huffing from her recent stair climbing and possibly from indignation. "I told you I was bringing that gun down here and was going to lock it in the silver cupboard. On account of the break-ins. Don't you remember?"

"Certainly I remember your saying that, but I asked you not to. I had discussed the subject with my father, and we had agreed we didn't want firearms about in the city, even under lock and key."

"I don't care to be doubted," Mrs. Hubbard retorted.

"No one doubts your good intentions, dear Mrs. Hubbard." Edith's voice softened, and she rose to look her old cook in the eye. "All I can say is that if you did bring the thing down, I knew nothing about it. I thought the matter was settled."

"Would Mr. or Mrs. Morris Watt be able to clear this up?" I asked.

Edith shook her head.

"They left on the Sunday before we packed up."

"What about you, Nita?"

"I wasn't there at all, sir."

"Nita had last Thanksgiving off to spend with her own family," Edith added.

The housemaid had been showing signs of recovery, but mention of her family started her juices flowing again.

"This is a hard day for all of us," said Mrs. Hubbard, hastening to drown out Nita's sniffles, "but I tell you again, missy, I don't very much like being contradicted to my face."

"Put it down to my bad memory then," Edith tactfully suggested. "As you say, we're none of us ourselves. Is that pastry I smell burning?"

"My pies!" Turning her bifocals reprovingly on me, the cook hastened off.

"I'm still not sure what this is about, Mr. Shenstone," Edith said. "I presume you've been looking for the gun in the silver cupboard and not finding it."

"It seems to me, Miss Watt, you've a very good idea what this is about."

"In that case, the quickest way to set your mind at ease is for someone to go to Roches Point and see if the gun is there."

Going or even phoning out of town meant expenses. The inspector would grumble. There had to be a simpler way to disqualify the Remington as the murder weapon. The position of Digby Watt's body suggested he had been facing his office building when he fell; if so, he had been shot at short range. A rifle was the wrong tool for the job, as well as being hard to conceal on city streets.

"This gun," I asked, "what size bullets does it fire? Your brother said you might know."

"Point three-five," Edith replied without hesitation.

I kicked myself all the way out to the motorcycle for not having asked sooner.

Chapter Seven

Olive Teddington lived with her aunt on Linsmore Crescent, farther into the eastern end of town than I normally have to go, but it wouldn't have been more than a fifteen-minute ride out the Danforth if a flatfoot hadn't taken a notion to pull me over. He objected to my riding on the sidewalk to get around a traffic snarl. Before I could show him my badge, he also drew my attention to the fact that I was leaking fuel and threatened to impound the motorcycle in a police garage. I mentioned, with a corroborative display of credentials, that someone had got in ahead of him. While his tone became more respectful, he still wanted to discuss the wisdom of spewing gasoline on pedestrians and pointed out that the inside of my right trouser leg was wet and that I had better not park any lit cigars in my lap. We did a proper inspection of the trapezoidal reservoir. This was an old machine, and I was beginning to understand why it hadn't been in great demand. A smallish rust hole at last presented itself as the most probable source of the problem. The constable, who like all constables hoped to make detective one day, donated his well-chewed wad of Doublemint as patching material. But by the time I set out again, I was feeling less jaunty and hoped I didn't stink too badly of gas to be questioning the young woman who might or might not have become the next Mrs. Digby Watt.

Crescents in Toronto come in every shape but semi-circular. Some meander; others form doglegs. Linsmore was a straight north-south street with jogs at the intersections and a pimple-shaped deviation in its lower end, as if someone had jostled the municipal draftsman's elbow. The house I was looking for was well north of this blemish, one of those new semi-detached three-bedrooms in the California bungalow style. You saw them going up all over town, each with its chilly front verandah and on the upper level half a dormer window jutting from a picturesque slope of shingles that hid the flat tarred roof behind.

There were no electric bells, and my knocking on Olive's door brought no response. Eventually I got a housewife in the other half of the semi to let me use her phone. When the operator put me through, the receiver was picked up after a couple of rings, but it was left to me to speak first.

"Miss Olive Teddington?"

By this time I was suspecting she had been given tranquillizers or sedatives to get her over the first shock of grief. There was a pause, and I was about to ask again.

"Yes."

That sounded awake enough, if grudging. Likely she had been hounded by journalists all day and was wary.

"My name is Paul Shenstone; I'm a detective sergeant. That was me knocking just now." I left her time to respond. She didn't. "I'm going to have to ask you some questions. Could you please come to the door?"

She hung up. But through the partition wall I heard shoes on the stairs, and she had the door open for me by the time I got to it.

I followed her into the living room, which, even with curtains open, the front verandah kept dim. Prickly plants in pots filled the windowsill. Olive sank onto a chesterfield in front of them with her back to what daylight there was.

I took it on myself to switch on a lamp before sitting, uninvited, in a wing chair.

My first good look at Olive showed her to be a plump girl with red hair pinned up in the back. In spite of her clear complexion, a pear-shaped face with heavy jaw and chin made her appear plain. Mourning can be flattering, but Olive's appearance was not improved by a shapeless, muddy-brown dress too long to be chic and too short to be elegant—although the sprig of lily-of-the-valley pinned to her bodice did add a note of freshness.

"I'm sorry to bother you today," I said.

She twisted her fingers and looked behind her out the window. She seemed an unlikely object of a millionaire's affections.

"Can you tell me, Miss Teddington, where you met the late Digby Watt?"

She gave no sign of hearing me.

"Olive?" I tried.

She looked at me now, her hazel eyes heavy with doubt.

"I understand you were close to Digby Watt. You must have had a terrible shock today. Would you like me to come back later?"

"No."

"You do want us to get to the bottom of Mr. Watt's murder, don't you?"

"I guess that's an important job for you. He was an important man."

Here was progress. Better sarcasm than the silent treatment.

"Some people look at it that way," I assented, "and I guess they'll be pushing me harder than usual. Personally, though—well, I'd be lying if I said I'm never impressed by wealth or power. But when someone is killed, I don't play favourites."

A bitter smile flickered across her face before she again looked over her shoulder at nothing.

"You say he was an important man, Miss Teddington. Was he important to you?"

She looked around as if the question caught her by surprise. "One way or another. Yes."

"I'd like you to talk about it," I said. "But wait, don't say anything yet. I'm guessing you or someone close to you had a bad experience with the police. A bad experience you put down to the fact that you or this person close to you wasn't a big shot. Am I guessing right?"

An indeterminate movement of the head.

A picked pocket, I thought, a break and enter where the value of the stolen goods was negligible by insurance company standards but significant to the Teddingtons. Jewellery that had been in the family. And the goods might not even have been insured. I could imagine how the complaint would sink to the bottom of the pile. The family would have been told that such crimes were rarely solved, advised to invest in better locks.

"I'm sorry that happened. All I can say is that that policeman wasn't me. But if you're afraid you can't trust me, you can ask anyone you like to sit in on our talk. Some one you can be sure will take your part. Would you like that?"

"No."

"The one thing I can't do for you," I continued, "is go away and not come back. Digby Watt has been shot down in the street. You knew him. I have to hear from you."

"I met him at church," she said. Her tongue sounded thick in her mouth. "Danforth Avenue United. I started going when I came to Toronto, in October."

"Came from where?"

"Hamilton. That's where I'd lived all my life before."

"Go on. How did you meet."

"I helped choose and arrange flowers when there was an occasion at the church. He noticed my fussing about. I didn't know who he was. He said a lot of complimentary things about my arrangements, and he started asking about the flowers, how much shade or sun or water different kinds like. Some questions I couldn't answer, but he didn't make me feel bad about not knowing. I guess I just thought he was a nice man who was a bit lonely."

"You knew what that was like," I said encouragingly. "You were new to the city and didn't have oodles of friends."

"I've never had what you would call oodles. Anyway, it got so if I was coming into the church on a Saturday to arrange the flowers for a wedding, he'd want to know about it and he'd come in and watch me. One Saturday when I was finished, he asked me if I'd like to go for a walk. He said I could bring someone else if I liked. Maybe he thought I'd be nervous about him. But I wasn't, so we started going for walks sometimes. And when we went for walks, he'd take me somewhere for tea. Or maybe he'd take me to hear a concert."

"What did he talk about?"

"Besides flowers? Often the church. Which were my favourite hymns. Which were his favourites. What the minister had said the Sunday before, and what I thought about it."

"Did he ever say anything to suggest he had enemies?"

Olive clenched her teeth. Something hostile flashed from her eyes before she could stop it.

"No, he never said a thing. He wanted me to believe he was just a nice old gentleman without an enemy in the world."

Perhaps, I thought, she's angry because she thinks if he had confided in her, she could have saved him.

"Were you thinking of marriage?"

"At one time I was. He was a lot older, of course, but as I say, I felt safe with him, and I thought maybe that was the important thing. Young men are usually louts. Besides, Digby made me feel special. He didn't just spend money on me; he told me I had lovely hair, lovely skin, that I was a lovely girl. The way he said those things I know he meant them. But then, lately, no. I wouldn't have married him."

"What changed?"

She was slow getting out an answer.

"I grew up," she said at last. "And I met his children. Just the once, but I know they wouldn't have wanted him to marry. After that, I didn't want to see him again."

"Did he propose?"

"No. I thought he was leading up to it, bringing me home and everything, but then again maybe he would have been happy just having things go on as they were."

"I haven't heard you express any grief or sorrow over his death, Miss Teddington."

"Haven't you?"

It occurred to me that the dun-hued dress might not be mourning at all, just her regular work clothes.

"You didn't go to the shop today, so I presume his death affected you strongly in some way. What *were* your feelings when you heard about it?"

"It's strange to have someone you once believed you knew get murdered. I thought a bit about our walks, and how at the time I didn't realize how little I really did know about him. But he wasn't a young man, and my aunt says the paper makes it sound like he died quickly. Did he?"

"I don't know," I said, the medical examiner's report notwithstanding. If Olive had anything on her conscience, it wasn't my job to make it easier.

"Whoever shot him," she offered, "must have thought he had a reason. Still, I guess Digby didn't deserve to die more than a lot of other people. I can't say I cried."

"Did you have a reason for wanting him dead?"

"No."

"Can you think of anyone who might have?"

"Whoever he left his money to. Isn't that usually the way?"

"Did he give you to understand he was leaving any of it to you?"

"No, and I wouldn't have wanted it either."

I ran through some of my routine inquiries before returning to her change of feeling regarding Digby Watt. Olive said she had been at home with her aunt the previous evening from six o'clock on. She claimed she had never touched or even seen a firearm and didn't know whether a .25 was a small gun or a big one.

"And when did you last see Digby Watt?" I wanted to know.

"Last Sunday evening when he and his driver brought me back here from his house in Rosedale."

"That was when you met his children?"

"Yes."

"Did they insult you, Miss Teddington, look down on you?"

Again a long silence.

"I have a doozy of a headache," she admitted. "That's the reason I stayed home today."

I crossed the room and offered her my bottle of Aspirin.

"No. Thank you." She looked up at me and made her next words a kind of reproach. "That's *gentlemanly* of you."

"Were they stuck-up Rosedale snobs who tried to make you feel you came from the wrong side of the tracks? Was that what changed the way you felt about Digby Watt?"

"Think that if you like. Let's just say I realized that evening what a gap there was between Digby and me."

What more there was to it would have to wait. It was after six, and I still had to report to Inspector Sanderson. She said if I wanted to do something really kind for her, I could turn off the lamp and show myself out. I did both.

Chapter Eight

"About time, Paul. Do you have someone we can send to the gallows for this?" Detective Inspector Sanderson was belching pipe smoke and bearing down on my desk, not waiting till I'd had a chance to read the messages piled there.

One of them, I noted, was from Morris Watt, to the effect that the name of the union boss at the time of the Canada Ski and Snowshoe strike was Sam Godwin. I shuffled it to the bottom of the pile.

"You're not asking who did it, sir?"

"A prominent victim means someone has to pay and pay soon. If there's no arrest in the next forty-eight hours, it's a detective's head that will roll. But you do have some latitude, Paul. I don't object to your collaring the actual guilty party. Past practice suggests a killing within the family; modern politics makes assassination by a communist more likely. Take your pick."

"Your boy Cruickshank has left me a summary here of Digby Watt's will." I held up a sheet covered in painfully neat handwriting.

"Read it later. The salient point is that Morris Watt and his wife are left the house on Glen Road and the income for life on nearly half of Digby's estate."

"Amounting to...?"

"That remains to be calculated, but I understand the assets they'll have to live off will be worth above a million dollars. Maybe substantially above. Whatever the amount, it passes at the death of the surviving spouse free and clear to their heirs. Edith the same, with the family cottage substituted for the house."

"Huh. The old man didn't trust either of his kids not to squander the principal."

"You talked to Morris, Paul. Do you think he knew?"

"Possibly. He was pretty aware of being kept under Daddy's thumb. Can I get you a chair, boss?"

"I'm comfortable standing."

Well, stand then, I thought, and stop pacing in front of my desk.

"Who gets to decide how the wad is invested?" I asked.

"Morris and the lawyer are co-executors. It's not a bad deal, Paul. Quite inoffensive men have killed for a tenth as much."

"All right," I said. "Let's see how the case would go. Morris must have known he'd inherit something juicy. Digby Watt wasn't the sort to tell his son to go out and make it on his own. So he'd have had the motive of greed, and likely resentment at Daddy's control. Digby kept Morris from soldiering in France, then kept him dangling the last seven years with deferred promises of a position. Perhaps Morris had been looking forward to the old man's end. It was just a matter of time. With Digby courting, though, time was no longer on Morris's side. Morris says he didn't think his father would have married, but in his heart he mightn't have been so sure that a stepmother and a new, less favourable will weren't in his near future. So far, it adds up. Opening Dad's trousers doesn't fit quite so well, unless you suppose Morris had a screw loose."

The inspector's eyebrows bristled in disgust. "I don't like the indecent exposure aspect of this case. What's the city coming to that a man can't even get himself shot without sex coming into it?"

"Suppose Morris didn't like the thought of sex either," I offered. "Specifically the thought of his father with a girl his daughter's age. Maybe Morris saw Digby's late-life interest in Olive as deserving of a public shaming."

"He had motive enough without that," snapped the inspector. "Motive galore. And Morris was on the scene. He could have sabotaged the car himself—just to throw us off his track. Frankly, Paul, it's hard to make sense of the car part of this crime any other way. How long would Digby Watt have been left standing alone on the street, even if the car had been working?"

"Five minutes, according to Morris."

"There you are! What kind of gunman needs more time than that to get off three measly rounds?"

A long-winded one, I thought, but didn't say.

"Well, sir, Morris did seem interested in whether we could get fingerprints from the missing steering pin. Still, how will it sit with the Rosedale crowd to see one of their own hanged?"

"Morris hasn't earned their respect the way his father did. They wouldn't like the idea that their sons might rise against them, but they see Morris as too insignificant to have sprung from their own loins. They'll let him take his lumps. Of course, we don't want to get the wind up him until we're sure we can make it stick, but—as I say, Paul—blood ties..."

Sanderson paused for effect, but the effect was lost in the full-chorus katzenjammer of typewriters and telephones. Headquarters suite at City Hall was only slightly less crowded in the evening than the morning. Why couldn't the Detective Inspector have made us both a little more comfortable by inviting me into his office? The eccentricities of the high and mighty. I stood up to lessen the height difference.

"I bet his wife Lavinia thought they were going to inherit," I said. "She tried to make me believe Digby Watt killed himself. I pointed out that he would scarcely have wasted a bullet on the book."

"Unless as a result of a dying spasm. But he certainly wouldn't have shot himself from more than ten inches away, and at any shorter distance—even supposing smokeless nitrocellulose powder was used—grains would have been deposited on his suit around the bullet holes. The chemist has found nothing of the kind. Has, in fact, noted the absence of powder grains. You have his report on the clothes in that pile of yours." Sanderson relit his pipe. "Why would Mrs. Watt be raising the subject of suicide? Is it a hare-brained effort to divert suspicion from herself?"

"Hare-brained she may be, but the sabotaged car doesn't fit her style that I can see, and the newsman says the phone call that brought him to the scene was from a man."

"A conspiracy, then."

"It wouldn't have to be a conspiracy, sir. She may suspect Morris and be trying to steer us away from him."

"If you like."

But I couldn't leave well enough alone. "It's also possible, though, that her suicide theory springs from vanity. Digby Watt spotted her three or four years ago in Winnipeg and married her off to his son. Lavinia may think her father-in-law really wanted her for himself and after his wife's death was consumed by melancholy and world-weariness because the fair Lavinia was no longer available."

"Foolishness." Sanderson cleared his throat. "Is she that much of a knockout?"

"I wouldn't sacrifice any vital organs for her, but you might have a different opinion, sir."

"What about the daughter Edith? She inherits big too."

I thought about Edith, but didn't feel like sharing any of my thoughts with the inspector. Edith struck me as strong-willed and more resentful of her father's relations with Olive—or of what she imagined those relations to be—than she cared to let on. A murderess? If homicidally inclined, she'd have been more likely to do away with Olive than with her father. *Unless* she saw Digby as bound and determined to marry one Olive or another.

"I think I need more time with Edith before saying what she's capable of."

"Come on, Paul," Sanderson continued maliciously. "These modern girls are capable of anything. I bet they think nothing of crawling under a car and removing a piece of the steering linkage."

"Any servants mentioned in the will?" I asked.

"The cook Hubbard is named to get a pension. Bequests of a fixed amount, enough to get them reestablished, go to any male servants in his employ at the time of his decease, and a smaller amount to any female servants."

"The chauffeur, Curtis Ritter, has a record we should look up, though he claims he never used firearms. At least his fingerprints will be on file. To be thorough, we should check up on the previous chauffeur too, a man called Thomas Webster. Maybe he didn't leave on as friendly terms as they say."

"Make a note of what you want in that line, Paul, and I'll have Knight or Howarth look into it."

"With pleasure, sir. As for the women, I can't see either of them doing it. The cook is verging on senility, but seems in no hurry to be pensioned off. And what the housemaid wanted most was for Digby Watt to help reconcile her parents to her marrying Curtis. Digby's death means no help and probably no marriage."

"Don't let the romance blind you," Sanderson warned. "It seems to me the maid's and chauffeur's combined legacies would finance a tidy elopement."

"I'm not putting Curtis in the clear, boss: he bears watching. But if Nita had any hand in the murder, she has the Gishes beat for acting."

"I'm sure there's a lot of new talent out there. What about the lady friend?"

"Olive Teddington."

"Not a name I saw among the heirs. Do you rule her out as well?"

"I don't know," I said. "She seems pretty miffed with Watt. Feels, I figure, that he misled her, posed as a simple old church-going nobody, then had her round to Glen Road, where he stood revealed as Mr. Moneybags. That's scarcely a motive for murder, though."

"No indeed. Some girls would have been pleased, at least till they found out the rich fiancé had died before changing his will."

"They weren't engaged, sir. She would have considered it at one time, she says, but not after that visit to his hearth and home last Sunday. There's probably more to her grudge than feeling made a monkey of."

"Let's look at the Bolshevik angle. Digby Watt was capitalism personified. We're not accustomed to red violence in the streets of Toronto, but one has to keep an open mind. Move with the times. You've a note there about a labour leader. Knight and Cruickshank came up with the same name when they were asking questions up and down Bay Street. Get onto that, Paul."

"Sure." I turned over in my mind the possibility that Olive might be a radical, resentful of anyone with two cents to rub together, but for now I had enough to follow up. "Can I assume we still have no eyewitnesses, no cartridge cases, and no weapon?"

"And nothing as regards the bullets but the calibre. If it's a revolver, the cases would have been carried away in the gun."

"I don't know of any .25 revolvers," I said.

"Neither do I," Sanderson admitted. "I've been trying to hurry up the autopsy all day, but I'm told we won't have anything till late tonight or tomorrow morning. Yes, Lindstrom."

The stenographer seemed surprised to have his approach noticed so promptly. There was a quaint fussiness about the man that reminded me of a rabbit.

"Phone call for the sergeant, sir." Lindstrom's nose twitched. "A Miss Edith Watt."

"Take it, Paul," said Sanderson. "I'm prepared to grant you a good deal of latitude in your conduct of this case. Just remember the clock is ticking. Your day's work isn't over, not by a long shot. I want to hear from you last thing before you go to bed tonight and the later the better."

"Did you want to give me your home phone number, sir?"

"I'll be here," Sanderson answered grimly.

"Inspector," I said, "if this is such an important case, why didn't we have a detective at the crime scene last night? I should say, the two crime scenes—the sidewalk outside 96 Adelaide West and the roof of Braddock's Garage."

Sanderson's scowl was such that I believed he now really was going to send me to blazes.

"Very well, I'll tell you. And then the subject is closed. Not to be referred to again. Last night, Detective Sergeant

Fergus was on his way to 96 Adelaide West when he suffered a stroke. The cab driver took him to the Toronto General Hospital. I wasn't notified till seven thirty this morning, by which time the crime, as you know, was far from fresh. Wilf can't speak yet, but he'll live—in retirement. This was the big crime he had been waiting for all his career, and when it finally came along, the thrill was too much for him. You can imagine how delighted I wasn't."

"I'm sorry about Mr. Fergus," I said.

"Yes, yes. We're all sorry about him, and sorry for him. But I decided this morning I was not about to take that chance again with another of the old guard. You're their equal in rank and, when sober, the fittest detective sergeant I have. Now pick up that bloody phone."

I did so, using the mouthpiece to cover a smile.

"Yes, Miss Watt, this is Paul Shenstone."

"Mr. Shenstone, I've a suggestion to make regarding the rifle." It was one of those voices that made a telephone connection sound clearer. "Have you done anything about checking up on it yet?"

"Is it still a Remington Model 8 Autoloading .35?"

"Point *two*-five—Morris found a record of it somewhere. Does it make a difference?"

That cured my grin.

"Somewhat," I replied with heroic mildness. "If you have a caretaker up there with a key, you could have him let one of the local constables in to have a look for it."

"Curtis will drive me up, and I'll let *you* in—or a policeman from East Gwillimbury, if you're too busy."

"Were you thinking of going tomorrow morning?"

"No, this evening. My father has been murdered, after all."

"Are you at home, Miss Watt?"

"Positively."

"I'll phone you back within the hour."

Rich girls, I thought. I was supposed to be speaking to Sam Godwin. After calling all the possible wrong numbers, I concluded he was not a telephone subscriber. I checked his last known address and found he wasn't in the city directory either. I phoned the Mounties, who make a point of keeping track of radicals. The sergeant I talked to started by saying that any request such as mine, involving national security and all, would have to be made through my chief. Even after some ice breaking chit-chat, he couldn't promise me anything before morning. It was going to take the better part of a day to run Brother Godwin to earth. At the same time, if I left checking for the gun till tomorrow, I would have to prevent anyone else from getting to it first. Edith or another family member might well drive up to Roches Point on their own. I phoned her back.

"Will you ride with us?" she asked, "or do police rules require you drive your own car?"

I didn't think the ancient motorcycle would make it. Besides, riding with her would give me the opportunity to question her further.

"How soon can you pick me up at police headquarters?"

"You won't have had supper, Mr. Shenstone. Am I right?"

"In this instance."

"Well, don't. I'll have Mrs. Hubbard pack us something to eat on the way up, and we'll be at City Hall in forty-five minutes. Please don't wait on the sidewalk. The sight of you there would echo unpleasantly."

Chapter Nine

I had no intention of waiting on the sidewalk. I wrote the note Sanderson had requested regarding the chauffeurs and suggested Knight or Howarth visit Stone's Garage on Bloor East as well, to get their slant on Curtis and see whether the Gray-Dort had been worked on there. The rest of the forty-five minutes I filled with listing names and phone numbers of various labour and left-wing political organizations that might have heard of Sam Godwin. Their offices were closed for the day, so I didn't feel I was being taken from urgent work when Edith Watt came asking for me at the front desk.

I can't say I was as indifferent as I pretended to the envious winks and glances I got from the other men in the office. As for Edith, well, they were public servants and knew enough not to leer, but the goofy looks they gave her made me just as glad Curtis wasn't there to take offence, or to have his respect for the law further undermined. I guessed his duty to stay with the motor was reinforced in this instance by a reluctance to show his face in police stations.

The Austin Seven Chummy could never have been meant to be a chauffeur-driven car. It seated four snugly, or in this case three and a family-size wicker picnic basket. The two-hour trip barely proved adequate for the consumption of cold chicken, potato salad, coleslaw and dinner rolls, followed by jam tarts and gingersnaps. I found the lemonade a cruel trial: all the while I was sipping it, I could feel my flask inside my jacket pocket, but could not unobtrusively get it near my lips. Edith had put me in the left front seat beside Curtis, who was compelled to drive this English toy from the right. She occupied the back with the supper, which she passed forward to me in manageable instalments. Curtis said he'd eat when we got there.

Night fell almost as soon as we left, so very little of the transition from city to suburb to farmland was clearly seen on the way north. The villages of Sharon and Queensville were points of light we passed through and left in our dust as the four-cylinder buggy trundled up the almost empty road at its leisurely cruising speed of forty miles an hour.

"Miss Watt," I said, addressing her over my shoulder between bites, "what do you think of the idea that a communist shot your father?"

"I think the fact that he was killed on a public street suggests something like that, a political rather than a personal motive. But then the murderer could have killed him that way to cover his traces. And aren't these political gestures usually accompanied by some indication of what they're all about? A hammer and sickle should have been painted on the front of his building, for example. Or some one should have phoned to boast and gloat. Has anyone done that?"

"Not that I know of. Not yet." Officially, I shouldn't have been giving out any information about the investigation, but I was enough befuddled by my first solid food of the day not to be able to see under what circumstances I might regret saying this much.

"Mostly he was thought a good employer," she continued, "but to a revolutionary that's worse than a bad, isn't it? Misleads the workers."

"Are you a student of Marxism, Miss Watt?"

"I'm a student of music, and not much of a one at that. My mother was the one who pushed singing lessons on me, so I haven't been pushed for two years. Really I'm just a spoiled dilettante who pokes her nose into all kinds of reading—uplifting and otherwise."

To be heard above the throbbing engine, she was leaning well forward in the back seat, her lips so close to my ear I could feel her breath.

"What do you sing?" I asked. "Any show tunes?"

"Art songs. In German mostly."

This didn't sound too appetizing, so I asked her to tell me more about her mother. I thought I might probe further Edith's feelings about her father's possible remarriage. Besides, I had to keep her talking if I didn't want the balmy breeze on the right side of my face to die down.

Edith described to me a more or less conventional late Victorian woman—born Dorothy Summers, raised in a small town, member of her church choir. Her marriage to Digby Watt had been a love match. She had adored her children and hoped for grandchildren until taken by influenza in 1924. She dedicated much time to her garden and, like her husband, to charities. Unlike her husband, she was fond of animals and made sure, despite Digby's objections, that Edith got the horse and riding lessons the girl craved. Digby had thought a car more practical.

I noted this minor conflict between father and daughter in which Dorothy Watt had made sure Edith prevailed.

"Do you still ride, Miss Watt?"

"No. I loaned Tut to a friend who broke his leg. He had to be euthanized."

"Which?"

"The horse—King Tut. The friend I flayed alive."

The car engine slowed and sputtered up a long hill towards Aurora.

"Quite apart from the question of age," I said when we'd safely reached the brow, "were you offended at the idea of Olive's taking your mother's place? Possibly eclipsing her memory?"

"All of that, Mr. Shenstone, certainly. But I loved my father too and wanted him to be happy. We all have nobler selves and baser selves, don't you think?"

The word "noble" gives me the pip. I had thought it and all its tribe had died a well-earned death ten years back. But it wasn't lost on me that this was the second time Edith had talked as if she harboured dual personalities.

"My nobler self," she continued despite my silence, "believed nothing would eclipse Dad's memory of Mum. I believe even if he had married Olive, he would have seen his partnership with her as something completely different."

"He brought her over to Glen Road last Sunday."

"Yes, he wanted her to meet his family. I was glad to see she wasn't a great beauty, to see that his head hadn't been turned by shallow glamour."

"What did you think of her otherwise?"

"Very shy at first, overawed by the house. I'm afraid Dad was a little disingenuous about how we lived, and I guess she doesn't follow the papers, so she had no idea. Once she took it all in, she was even angry. Well, she's red-headed, so perhaps you can expect hot temper. I don't doubt Dad would have smoothed it all over with her had he lived."

"You didn't like her. Admit it."

"I tried to like her. She seemed interested in the house, so I offered to show her around a bit. Lavinia didn't feel like coming, so Morris and Dad kept her company. While we were upstairs, Olive asked me where the money for all this came from, and I mentioned a few of the companies Dad had started and made a go of—Wellington Pork and Poultry, Atkins Hardware, Peerless Kitchen Appliances. She asked if that was the same as Peerless Armaments, and I said that during the war the factory in Hamilton had switched over from stoves to shells. I thought I heard her gasp a bit at that, so I said, 'Are you a pacifist, Miss Teddington?'"

"And?"

"She replied that, on the contrary, she had munitions workers in her family. And then she commented on some old photographs on the wall of the upstairs corridor, and we never got back to the subject. Strange, now I think of it. I still don't know why she gasped like that."

I very nearly gasped myself. I was wondering if members of Olive's family could have made the defective shell that killed Horny Ingersoll...

"Do you recall anything else that was said that evening?" I asked at last.

"After the tour of the house, and a cup of tea in the conservatory, Olive said quite abruptly that she wished to go home, that it didn't do for a young woman to be out late. It sounded as if she were scolding us for something, but I couldn't quite make sense of it, and I suppose she was still angry at Dad for not telling her earlier how he lived. Anyway, he didn't seem to think anything of her remark. He just called Curtis and accompanied her home."

I turned to Curtis.

"What did Digby Watt and Olive Teddington talk about on the drive from Glen Road to her aunt's house last Sunday evening?"

"I don't know," said Curtis.

"You told me you thought highly of Digby Watt, Curtis.

Your discretion, which I'm sure he valued as long as he lived, can now only obstruct the investigation of his murder."

"Mr. Shenstone," Edith interjected, "Curtis was driving the Gray-Dort that evening. He couldn't have heard what the passengers were saying."

"Is that so, Curtis?"

"Yes."

"Is there a sliding glass screen between the driver's seat and the passenger seats?"

"Yes, there is," Edith again answered for the chauffeur.

"And was that screen open or closed on the drive to Olive's home last Sunday? Curtis?"

"I couldn't hear what was said."

"Was the screen open or closed?" I sensed Edith leaning forward to again intervene. "Let him answer please, Miss Watt."

"I didn't notice," said Curtis. He seemed to be driving faster.

"Curtis, stop the car," I said.

"Do as he says, Curtis," said Edith.

The car came to a smooth stop on the side of the dark country road.

"Kill the engine, please."

Suddenly there was no sound but the creak of branches from a roadside tree, the rustle of new leaves, and the hiss of the cooling radiator.

"Now, Curtis," I said. "Was the screen closed or open? And don't say you didn't notice, because you notice everything about your employer's cars. You take great pride in keeping track of every detail."

"It was open."

"That's better. And did you hear what conversation passed between the late Digby Watt and Miss Olive Teddington?"

"Even with the slide open, Mr. Shenstone," Edith said, "the back seat is far enough back that with the engine noise the driver can't hear what's said in an undertone. I've driven that car, and I know."

Edith had a hand curled over the leather back of each of the front seats. The pale oval of her face was thrust forward between Curtis and myself. It was possible she had something to hide, but I thought it more likely that she was just following the employer's code of protecting her people, and was really bursting with curiosity. Perhaps she had even tried asking these questions herself and been stonewalled.

"Miss Watt," I said, "it's been a long day, and there's still work to do. You cannot speed matters up by speaking for Curtis. He's quite able to speak for himself."

She sat back six inches at that.

"When they conversed quietly," said the chauffeur, "I couldn't hear. When I pulled up in front of her aunt's house, however, Miss Teddington raised her voice."

"And said?"

Curtis seemed to look to Edith for permission.

"Go on," she told him. "Let's get to the bottom of this."

"Miss Teddington said, 'You killed my sister. I never want to see you again.'"

"The girl's dippy!" Edith exclaimed. "Perhaps dangerously so. What happened then?"

"Then—" Curtis spoke slowly and dully, as if unaware he'd said anything sensational. "—she got out of the car before I could open the door for her, and she ran into the house."

Edith whistled a falling note. "Good riddance, I say."

"How did Digby Watt take all that?" I asked.

"He just said, 'Home please, Curtis.' Then he pulled the slide closed. I drove him home."

"Did he subsequently refer to the incident?"

"No."

"Did he to your knowledge ever see Miss Teddington again?"

"No."

"Did you ever see her again?"

"No."

"Thank you, Curtis," I said. "Drive on, please."

Curtis drove on and soon brought the little car to rest again before a pair of white wooden gates, closed but not locked. He got out and opened them, propping each with a metal spike that swung down from the bottommost crossbar.

"Did you know you inherit this cottage and its contents, Miss Watt?" I asked while Curtis was out of the car.

"No. Thanks for telling me. That makes it easier."

Curtis got back in and drove the car through. When he stopped on the other side, I intended to ask what she meant, but she leaped out and helped Curtis reclose the gates before we proceeded up the curving drive. The headlamps swept over an arc of bordering hedge. Then we swung round into a gravel parking area in front of a white frame two-storey house. Curtis asked if he should accompany us inside, with an emphasis that made it clear he thought Miss Watt needed a protector. She insisted he remain in the car and eat his supper. She would call if she needed him. Practically bounding up the few steps of the unscreened verandah, she took a ring of keys from the pocket of her stylishly pleated spring topcoat and let herself into the cottage. With the sure-footedness of long acquaintance, she picked her way through the dark ground floor. I kept up as best I could, arriving in the kitchen just in time to see her pull the electrical master switch. The lights that came on weren't too hard on our eyes. Bulbs of low wattage behind ochre shades picked out the dark cedar-panelled corridor and staircase that led us to Digby Watt's bedroom.

"Don't touch it," I barked as I caught Edith groping in a closet.

"I already have," she said, "just at the end. But it's there. Looks like Mrs. Hubbard misremembered."

"Mind if I take it away and have it examined?"

"You don't mean you think someone might have killed Dad with it and put it back here? No stone unturned, I suppose. Go ahead."

I used my handkerchief to lift the rifle by its muzzle from the corner of the closet. It was indeed a .25. From it I carefully removed and pocketed a box magazine—currently empty—that when loaded would allow up to five shots in quick succession. If this were the murder weapon, Digby Watt might have been shot from some distance, might never have even seen his attacker. But in that case, the body would have had to have been turned around after it fell. For what purpose?

A dry, cracking sound jerked me back to the present.

Edith had gone out onto a boarded-up sun porch and, when I found her there, was rummaging through a battered secretary desk. A fierce-looking chisel and splinters of wood lay on the writing surface.

"Was the key to that not on your ring?" I asked.

"Don't know where Father kept the key," she said, "but you tell me I'm the owner now."

"After probate. What did you find?"

"An exercise book with Dad's writing in it and some letters. I'm hoping they'll give us a clue as to why he seemed gloomy the last few months. I already looked through his papers at Glen Road and found nothing. Now, is there anything else you'd like to see here? If not, we can start back."

This girl was something new in my experience.

"Are you constituting yourself a detective, Miss Watt?"

"A detective sergeant, I think," she tossed back. "Isn't that better?"

"Evolution's crowning glory," I agreed.

I looked through the desk and found nothing of interest apart from the documents Edith had already removed. She led the way, first back to the kitchen where she disconnected the electricity, then out to the waiting car.

She suggested we leave the picnic basket in the front, where it had been moved for Curtis's benefit, and that I join her in the back so that we could go over the new evidence together. Wanting to make sure she destroyed or sequestered nothing, I fell in readily enough. I won't pretend it wasn't a squeeze. The back seat was built for two, but only two children could have sat there without pressing against one another, and two men my size would not have fitted at all. There was no trunk, so the rifle lay under our feet. We read by the light of a flashlight borrowed from Curtis's tool kit. The chauffeur, guardian of appearances, disapproved of the arrangement first to last, but could make no headway against Edith. Sullenly, he wiped the last traces of supper from his mouth, turned the car around, and began the drive back to Toronto.

"Why would he have left his diary at the cottage?" I asked.

"I'm as surprised as you, Mr. Shenstone, but for a different reason. He didn't normally keep a diary at all. Let's see what it says. Shall I read aloud?"

"Keep your voice down," I cautioned, with a glance at

the back of Curtis's neck. "I'll be following along."

"Done. Here goes: *July 5, 1925. Received a disturbing letter yesterday, forwarded from the city, from an ex-serviceman calling himself Robert Taylor. I'm not sure how to respond. Perhaps no answer is best, as the writer is very upset, possibly unhinged from shell shock. There's no one in the family I feel like talking this over with. Mustn't show the children, especially Morris, any sign of weakness. Morris needs to build up his self-confidence, and that cannot be done by letting him entertain any doubts about the ethical basis of our enterprises. Perhaps, though, I can talk the matter out with myself here, despite not having the journal habit. Too much self-analysis breeds unhealthy and unproductive doubts. Dorothy gave Morris a blank book to keep a journal when he was in his teens. I quietly made the book disappear and bought him a ledger book in its place.* How horrid of Daddy!"

As Edith flung the scribbler down on her knees, a folded piece of inexpensive note paper slipped from between the pages.

"Is that Robert Taylor's letter?" I said. "I'd like to read it before you go any further. Better still, I'll take all these documents to the station. That's the proper place to examine their contents."

"Without my presence?"

"This is police business, Miss Watt." I sounded stuffy to myself, and felt that it was a little late to be playing this card, but I had a strong premonition of what was coming, and I knew I didn't want that premonition confirmed while sitting thigh to thigh with Digby Watt's maiden daughter and inhaling the floral scent of her shampoo.

"These are my documents, Mr. Shenstone."

"After probate."

"Are you pretending they're yours till then? I'm not letting you take them without a warrant. Now if you want to know what Robert Taylor says, listen up. No date. *Dear Mr. Peerless, If the Boche had won the war, they'd have given you a medal. I served in an 18-pounder gun battery. In 1915, as we were laying down a barrage in the second battle of Ypres, one of your bad shells killed one of our men, a good Canadian gunner valuable to the war effort and a human being with a right to expect better of his own countryman. More than that, Horner Ingersoll was a special friend of mine. If you want to know what happened to him, he had his...* Oh, God."

"Give that to me."

"Don't pull! Don't: you'll rip it. Just read silently along as you said."

Silently I read: *...he had his balls blown off and then just bled to death. Killed by a punk shell painted up to pass inspection. I want you to think about that, Mr. Peerless. I've been thinking about that for ten years now from 1915 to 1925, and I'm tired of carrying that thought alone. I haven't had much good fortune since the war, while you dirty profiteers have just gone on making one fortune after another. So you think how lucky you are to have your wealth and your genitals and your sleep at night, because after the rotten ammunition you sent us, I'd say you don't deserve any of them. Worst wishes, Robert "Tinker" Taylor.*

There it was, a second member of Horny's battery liable to be suspected of killing Digby Watt. Ivan and now Tinker. I did not in the least like where this case was leading.

"Finished?" said Edith, blowing her nose vigorously. "I don't really understand the part about bad shells, but let's go on with the diary and see if it's explained there. I'll read aloud. No, don't make difficulties. Anything Dad wrote, I can say. *Taylor refers to a time when the Empire had desperate need of shells, and there wasn't more than one factory in the Dominion that had any experience in their manufacture. We did our best under government direction and were given to understand that every shell we made would be inspected before shipment to London. Naturally, I never authorized any measure that would frustrate those inspections. As for profits during the war, we made much more on pork than on shells, but yes, we were paid. Were we supposed to do the work pro bono and pro patria while other firms whose product was no better were improving their balance sheet? Peerless management was overhauled as soon as I learned that our munitions were not meeting Imperial standards. By 1916, the problems had been fixed, and our shells misfired at no greater rate than those made in Britain or anywhere else. I wish I could say that the experience of Taylor and his companions was a unique one. It was, however, all too common for the period. What is unique is the rancour Taylor pours on my head. No one has ever written to reproach me in these terms. Am I not duty bound to report him to the police as a potential danger to himself and others? I tell myself all these things, and yet I cannot feel quite easy. Perhaps because, of all the injuries a man can suffer, injury there can never be portrayed as noble. It's a mercy poor Ingersoll died. Most war wounds evoke some sympathy; however, in a case such as his, sympathy would always have been tinged with contempt. I think I shall answer Taylor's letter. It's the responsible thing to do. All the same, great wealth is such a tremendous responsibility I sometimes question, God help me, if it's worth it. A fine state of affairs! At the very least, I should like to know someone for whom I am not Mr. Peerless, or Mr. Atkins Hardware, or Mr.*

Dominion Consolidated Holdings. I understand those monarchs of old who wished to walk among their subjects in disguise and pass for one of them, if only for an evening." Edith turned a page, fanned through the remaining pages. "Huh," she said. "The rest of the book is blank... Does this mean Peerless made shells that killed our own soldiers?"

"Yes."

"You knew?"

"Yeah."

"Could any of those shells have blown up in the factory?"

"Something could have," I said. "A shell. Powder. A fuse."

"So," said Edith sadly, "when Dad walked among the people in disguise and went looking for someone he could be himself with, he found Olive, whose sister was a munitions worker killed at the Peerless Plant."

"Possibly."

"There's another paper tucked in here, a carbon copy of Dad's reply to Robert Taylor. He must have typed it himself. *July 6, 1925. Dear Mr. Taylor, I can't tell you how sorry I am for your experience with a defective shell made at my factory. I could plead circumstances in my defence, but they would be of no comfort to you. We were guilty of what to you must always seem inexcusable carelessness. One of the great injustices is that wars are never waged by the men who declare them or the men who profit from them. With the wisdom of retrospection over the last dozen years, I am tempted to believe that the latter two types of men should not exist at all. In any case, had I been born a generation later, I should no doubt have given my youth on the altar of patriotism and, had I survived the carnage, should have felt no less bitter than yourself. I cannot restore to you either your sleep or your friend. Should you desire employment, however, now or in the future, I believe there is something I can do. Please write again without hesitation. Warmest regards, Digby Watt.* That was handsome of Dad."

"He seems," I said, "to have had a way with words."

"That's hardly fair. He wasn't smooth at all in the way you imply. I'm sure this was written from the heart."

Typed from the heart, I mentally corrected. That inexcusable carelessness business stuck in my craw. Sure, Digby Watt had been careless, I could buy that—so long as he didn't pretend it was the whole story. Someone acting in his name, after all, had been very carefully deceitful. But I didn't want to pick a quarrel with Edith on the day of her father's death.

"Is it likely he sent it?" I asked.

"You'll have to look Taylor up and ask him."

"Anything else in that packet?"

"Nothing."

"Now that you've had a chance to read it all, Miss Watt, will you let me borrow these documents and use them for any light they may shed on the investigation."

"Yes, of course..."

She gave me a softer look than I had seen before on her vital and energetic face—or perhaps it was just my fancy spreading its wings in the dim car. Her innocence was appealing and appalling. I turned away, towards the shadowy undulations of the countryside we were traversing, and confronted innocence here too. Here lay fields never cratered by artillery, fields in which no shells had exploded prematurely or lay unexploded and waiting to make new red entries in the balance sheet of a war long over.

"It's been a disturbing evening," Edith went on mildly, "but I couldn't bear the thought of sitting at home discussing funeral arrangements with Lavinia. And I'm glad to know something of the part of Dad he didn't care to show us. Even if we knew the names of his companies and Olive didn't, there was still so much he hid from us. It was how he thought a patriarch should behave. It was maddening, but I suppose it's foolish to be mad at history."

"We're all fools then," I said, looking out for a flare over no man's land.

Chapter Ten

No one thought Prohibition could last the year. It had already been repealed in every province west of Ontario, and the legalization of weak beer—while it pleased no one—suggested the end was beginning. A sense of gloomy foreboding hung over the room in which I now sat as surely as over the Women's Christian Temperance Union, though not quite for the same reason.

The room in which I sat was the blind pig of Ernie and Dolores Lacombe, which occupied the loft of a disused stable in the eastern harbour industrial district. It was a neighbourhood of metal, oil, coal, cartage and construction companies, with a few lonely dwellings sprinkled in. Dolores—a sinewy woman in a checked shirt and dungarees—did the pouring, book-keeping, chatting and grumbling. Tonight as usual she did all these while jostling an infant on her left arm. Although the ceiling was collapsing, the lights flickered, there was no heat, and the whistling drafts persistently failed to dissipate the whiff of horse manure, she had no inclination in the present climate to invest in renovations. A few patrons had urged her to consider applying for a licence under the coming regime, but to that idea she scornfully replied through thin, tight lips—

"You think anyone would drink here by choice?"

"Sure, Dolores," I said, a second ounce of smuggled but sound Seagram's VO seeping amiably through my limbs, "you could clean the place up."

"Tell me another! Dirt's the only thing holding this building together."

"Is that a proverb? Mud's thicker than mortar?"

"Go on, Paul. Clean or dirty, it's still the waterfront. Handy to derelicts and deadbeats—while our present clientele moves uptown to sparkly new cocktail lounges."

"Don't kid yourself. Your clientele, myself included, will never see the inside of anywhere sparkly. Even when drink is legal, we'll still be riffraff. That's why I come, to enjoy the company of my kind."

"You come to get soused like anyone else," said Dolores, pouring me another drink.

The baby came awake, perhaps with the smell of the rye, and started to gurgle.

"Doesn't he, Peaches?" she cooed around her cigarette. "Soused."

Curtis had dropped me at police headquarters close to eleven thirty p.m. Not wanting to linger there and risk encountering the inspector, I handed the Watts' rifle to a constable for delivery in the morning to the university lab and made for Cherry Street.

"Dolores," I said, "have you heard anything about this Watt murder?"

"Heard he was left dead with nearly a hundred dollars in his pocket. The waste of that just sickens me."

"Gunned down in the street. That's a little out of Toronto's line. Is anyone bragging?"

"Not to me."

"Who do you suspect?"

"Nobody."

"We don't have the gun yet, a point two-five. Any ideas, Dolores?"

"None."

"Maybe I was wrong about the virtues of this place," I said. "It doesn't have the convivial atmosphere I've always associated with it."

"May's here."

Dolores looked out hopefully across the dingy room. There was a pretty fair turnout, maybe two dozen. Most were single men, of course, but there were couples too, and one or two unattached women trying to make ends meet or looking for adventure. Not, by and large, a rough crowd, but most had been in trouble with the law at one time or another. Sometimes the Lacombe children, as many as five of them, up to twelve years old, were hanging about. Seeing them usually got me talking to Dolores about the Children's Aid Society. But for tonight the tadpole in the pink blanket—now slumbering again—was the only representative of the younger generation, and I let it be.

There was no band or piano, just a wind-up gramophone fed one of a dozen discs in random rotation by Dolores's husband Ernie, an obese man in red suspenders. It was said that a chunk of Krupp's shrapnel in his head had left him simple, a perpetual seven-year-old in a body now approaching forty. Two couples were shuffling about a stretch of open floor without much dash. If the jazz age had any glamour, it was not to be found this night in the Reliable Cartage Company's stables.

May must have been in one of the curtained-off cubicles along the far end wall.

"Maybe later," I said. "In the meantime, I'm looking for a gun."

"Long gun or revolver?"

"I don't know. Maybe neither."

"Jesus."

Dolores spat into the sink she had had installed. It had

no trap, its main purpose being the quick disposal of hooch in the event of a raid. Her hands were scarred from the cuts she had suffered while breaking bottles there. Raids were no longer frequent, but still a possibility.

"Look, Paul, I appreciate your understanding and discretion and forbearance in view of how this place isn't strictly lawful, and you're welcome to all the whisky you can drink, but I can't 'assist the police with their inquiries', as they say, without more to go on than that."

"Let's say a pistol. There are lots of .45 or .38 service revolvers floating around since the war, as well as far too many people who've been taught how to fire them. But our killer didn't use anything so military. Where would he go for a tidy little .25 vest-pocket automatic?"

"Beats me."

The unaccustomed rattle of a ukelele interrupted our talk. I looked up to see three new arrivals. The two men wore casual rather than work clothes, and their haircuts looked expensive. They were well built, perhaps Varsity footballers come slumming for a thrill, and likely thought they could take care of themselves. I'd spent a few months on campus myself and more or less recognized the type. They had a coed with them in a long, loose cardigan and short tartan skirt. She really could shimmy and Charleston, as she showed with one of the cakeaters while the other went to town on his little instrument.

Uncertain how Ernie would take the competition, I prepared if there were trouble to back him up. Though I have to say I preferred the college kids' taste in music. Ernie favoured the yearning ballads: "The Man I Love," "It Had to Be You," "Someone to Watch Over Me," and "What'll I Do?" The newcomers went in for the songs with the liveliest rhythms combined with the silliest lyrics:

"Tea for Two," "If You Knew Susie," "Yes Sir, That's My Baby," "When the Red, Red Robin Comes Bob, Bob, Bobbin' Along." Ernie looked up at the furious strumming and sniffed the air. He saw that the regulars appreciated hearing a few different tunes. He didn't yank "Always" off the turntable, but when it had run its course, he took a break and just sat watching the dancers.

I followed his gaze. That's when I saw May, in one of those red Chinese sheaths with the high collar and the slit skirt. She was dancing with a powerfully-built man I hadn't noticed before. He wore an oilskin jacket the colour of storm clouds and a greasy woollen toque. He was trying to kiss her, but she kept brushing him off. Then he stopped dancing, took her face in both his meaty mitts, and planted his mouth willy-nilly on hers. She must have bit his lip or maybe even his tongue, for he broke away with a cry of "Bitch!" A second later, there was an unsheathed knife in his hand. Five-inch blade, double-sided. It was no toy. May backed away, holding before her her small white beaded reticule. From it, as she backed, she drew a small black automatic pistol. She pointed it at the man's belly and flicked off the safety with her thumb.

Other patrons had been moving in to simmer things down, but hesitated when they saw the pistol. I brushed by them and got between May and the man. I couldn't quite put away the fear of a slug in the back if her finger were to slip on the trigger, but he scared me more.

"No knives on Tuesdays," I said in a nice placid voice. "Put it on the floor."

"If you're this slut's fancy man, you should thank me for breaking her to service."

I would have felt more comfortable if he'd been drunk, but his deep voice was unslurred, his eye clear, his feet firmly planted. He appeared to have come for other pleasures. I intended he should look for them elsewhere.

"For now," I said, "I'm the bouncer."

That's when he rushed me. Don't let anyone tell you that when a man charges you that way you should try to grab the wrist of his knife hand. You'll get your own wrist slit, and your throat soon after. I picked up a chair and whacked him across the face with it. He took it better than I'd have liked and with his left hand even managed to grab one of the chair rungs. As I felt him pull, I pushed, ramming the legs into his chest. That's when he lost patience and threw the knife. He was too much on his back foot. The blade came at me high—too high for my vitals, that is, though if I hadn't dodged I might have caught it in the eye. Well, he only had one knife, and once he'd parted with it we were even. He was still bigger than I am, but I had hurt him some, and blood from the gash my chair had opened in his forehead was getting into his eyes. Before he could wipe them, I moved in and got a fist on his jaw, then another. He tottered, throwing blind punches that didn't bother me much. Meantime, I hit him again. He went down. While he was lying there, I made an overture—

"If you leave, we can stop this."

"Yeah, get out!" said Ernie.

I heard nothing but assenting voices and lots of them. Even the college kids chimed in, observing what a shame it was that some folks couldn't handle ukelele music.

I guess he saw he was licked. Of course, he tried to reclaim his knife from where it was sticking in the wall. I got to it first.

"I'll chuck it out the window when I see you in the street," I said.

He didn't believe me, but I was as good as my word. I

went to the window and drew back the thick curtains. When he appeared below, I threw the knife at the nearest telephone pole. The blade buried itself in the wood, ten feet above his head. He went away cursing. I let the curtains drop.

May came towards me. Her dyed blonde hair was worn in a bob as smooth as a helmet, and her short, plump body was flatteringly elongated by her floor-length oriental gown. It was as shiny red as a fire truck. As she approached, the slit skirt showed a stretch of pale, round leg above white high-heeled pumps. Her pencilled eyebrows were always thin and dark and never seemed to follow the same line from one time I saw her to the next. Sometimes they turned down at the inside edge, up at the outside; sometimes they formed asymmetrical curves. Tonight they seemed to be at their best, etched with black severity—yet in a moderate, uniform arc—just below her yellow bangs and above her dark eyes. Half way down the right side of her nose, there was a mole that she always tried and—to my relief—never succeeded in powdering over. While her ex-partner and I were fighting, she had repaired her smudged makeup. Her lips and perhaps a little more of the area around her mouth were freshly painted a deep colour that did not quite match her dress, and a third red was represented by her nail polish. Her fingers were wrapped around the white-beaded reticule. The gun was nowhere to be seen.

"Buy you a drink?" I said, as we both sat down.

Dolores was already setting before May a glass of what the establishment liked to call champagne, as well as another few ounces of rye for me.

"Your health, May," I said. "How's every little thing?"

"Fine and dandy. Dirt washes off."

"Bullets don't. I didn't know you went armed."

"Now you do."

"Funny thing is, I came here tonight to ask about guns. You wouldn't know Digby Watt?"

"'B what?' Is this a riddle?"

"The businessman who was shot down in the street last night."

"Oh, him. He had no business with me."

"We can't find the gun, maybe a gun like the one you've got in your handbag there."

"You're not serious, Paul." She clutched the bag more tightly.

"He was a widower with a weakness for very young women."

"Thanks. I guess. But you know where I was last night."

"For part of it. I can't say I noticed which part."

"Banana oil."

She was right about that. May hadn't killed Watt, and I'd no thought of pretending she had. But a gun like hers was another matter. Vest-pocket pistols might be common as fleas in foreign parts. Not here. Apart from anything else, I wanted to scare her a bit about keeping a thing like that around.

"Could I see it?" I asked.

"It? Oh, the gun. As long as you don't really suspect me." She looked around, unlatched the bag and tipped it onto the table. The black semi-automatic slipped out like a rotten tooth. "It's only for self-protection, cross my heart."

It was just over four inches long with a grip too short for me to get even two of my fingers around. The metal was soft and poorly finished. A medallion containing a jut-jawed man's crowned head adorned each grip. The inscription on the left side read *Prince, Cal. 6.35 .25"*

Eibar. Spain exported some first-rate guns—but this was not one of them. It was, rather, one of the innumerable Spanish cheapies, sloppily assembled from non-standardized parts that made for weapons that were liable to jam and a nightmare to trace.

"I'll need to see your permit too."

"Poor you." She patted my knee consolingly, her hand spilling over onto my inner thigh. "It's not even mine. I'm just borrowing it."

"Makes no difference." I had dropped any hint of a bantering tone. I didn't feel nearly as happy winking at illegal firearms as at illegal drinks. Turning the gun over, I pushed back a catch at the rear of the butt and popped out the magazine. It was charged with three of a possible six rounds of Automatic Colt Pistol ammunition. To see if there were a round in the chamber, I gripped the top rear of the pistol and drew back the slide. Another round there, which I removed. So the number of missing bullets equalled the number that had perforated Watt's waistcoat. "How long have you had this?"

"You sound like the juvenile judge when I was first caught kissing boys' cocks."

"How long?"

"Couple of inches—just *little* boys. Oh, you mean how long have I had the...? A week, I guess, maybe less."

"Has it been out of your possession at all during that time?"

"What good's it to me out of my possession? No."

"When was it last fired?" I sniffed the mechanism, but could smell nothing but oil.

"Not since I've had it."

"There are only four of a possible seven bullets here."

"I don't expect to need as many as four."

"May, it's dangerous for you to have this. Where did you get it?"

"Go fish."

"Look, if you've never used this gun, you don't know how it fires. Even if the thing were decently made, it could go off by accident and kill you. You could die in a shootout. Or you could kill someone, the way you almost did tonight—and, whether the law punished you or not, you'd have to live with blood on your hands. Not everyone's cut out to be a killer, May. Any loony bin could show you vets who found that out the hard way. Those would be the risks of your carrying the Rolls-Royce of pistols. But you're not dealing with a fine instrument here. These Eibar guns are junk, thrown together for quick sale. You'll be lucky if it doesn't blow up in your hand."

May shrugged. As if to say life's always a gamble. As if to say I embarrassed her when I sounded too much as if I cared.

"And besides," I added, "carrying this gun without a permit could land you in jail for three months."

"If it does, you're no gentleman. We have a deal."

"Whatever deal we have doesn't cover guns. Where did you get it?"

"From a date."

"Who?"

"Think I know their names? You, for instance. I know your name isn't really Paul. But I don't know what it is, whether it's Fool, Moron, Idiot or Jerk."

"It's Paul. Describe this man of mystery."

"Let's see: two eyes, two feet, and somewhere in between..."

While talking she kept her hand in my lap and was nudging my leg under the table with her own. Her toilet water was strong in my nostrils, stronger than the taste of the whisky. I pushed my glass away.

"I'm seizing this gun," I said in a last attempt at being policemanly. Truly, I hoped I wouldn't have to trace it: it could have been brought a great distance by any of the sailors, truck drivers or railwaymen that drifted through the port and through May's bed. I tucked pistol and magazine into separate pockets.

"Anything you say...Paul." She moved closer. "You know, I was watching your expression when you opened up that slob's face with the chair. You enjoyed doing it, didn't you?"

It had been a long day, and the most taxing part of it physically had been sitting wedged against Edith in the back seat of the small swaying car for 120 minutes. I wanted to efface the memory, and neither the fight nor the whisky had done it. I was still wondering if Edith had squeezed my arm when I got out in front of HQ or whether that had been my imagination.

"I bet," May persisted, "that's the most fun you've had since you got out of bed this morning."

I ran my hand down the tight red bodice of her dress.

"Maybe it was," I said, "but I'm willing to try for a new record. Let's go somewhere less public."

"Just remember: I don't let anyone kiss me on the mouth."

She did, though. It was nice.

Intermezzo

When I got home from the war in April of 1919, I felt I ought to pay a call on Horny's parents, and yet it was the last thing in the world I wanted to do. Arthur Ingersoll sold tobacco and newspapers and, when I first met Horny, was making as good a job at it as could be made. By the time we both enlisted, Horny's father ran the shop in the King Edward, the newest and by far the ritziest downtown hotel. In my adolescence, I'd found him an overbearing man, not just because he whacked his kids—all fathers did that—but because of his sulks. He was a real speak-when-you're-spoken-to kind of parent. Being constantly exposed to news headlines made him feel he was better informed than anyone else, and so he did the talking in his home. He rarely wanted to hear other members of his family, let alone their callow friends, venture an opinion. Or even a fact. If he were angry about something, he wouldn't speak for days. On the other hand, he loved his two boys and one girl, never stinting on their education or anything that would further it. Perhaps this was money wasted in the case of Horny, who was no scholar. Arthur, however, was forgiving, and rather admired Horny's reputation as a lady-killer. His wife Gladys had been a Horner and had wanted her first son to carry that name. She was less happy with the tomcatting ways her son was allowed to develop, but was unable to stand up to her husband about this or anything else. On the very few occasions I had visited her home, she had been kind to me. Because I was quiet under the Ingersoll roof, I think she mistakenly saw me as a good influence on Horny. She hoped, she said, I would help him with his studies. When we enlisted, she said that since Horner wasn't much of a correspondent, I must write and give her her son's news. I tried to tell her we had enlisted in different branches of the service and wouldn't in the normal course of events be seeing much of each other. She said to write anyway—and I did, once or twice, before Horny's death. She actually sent me a pair of socks she had knitted for me, which I was able to use, and a loaf of her bread, which went mouldy before it reached me.

I can't tell you the number of times I circled the King Eddy Hotel that April. I hadn't been able to write to the Ingersolls since their first-born son had died, and yet I felt I had one final report to file. As it was really to Horny's mother I felt I owed this, in the end I avoided the King Edward altogether. Around four one spring afternoon, I went to the Ingersoll home.

On the way, I stopped to gawk at Winchester Street Public School with its tall, thin windows and to recall having swatted a baseball through one of them. From the school, nose twitching with the memory of chalk dust, I followed our childhood footsteps to a terrace of red-brick Victorian houses, the kind where ceilings are so high that a two-storey house is as tall as any three-storey built after the war. This was Toronto's mid-eastern neighbourhood of Cabbage Town, convenient to two cemeteries and to the city jail. And—of more interest to boys—near enough the Riverdale Zoo that we were able to hear the wolves howl at feeding time. A prestige address? Not everyone thought so. But residents suffered from no sense of inferiority.

Gladys answered my knock, looked me over twice before she recognized me, then gave me her old sweet smile. Her hair was greyer, her eyes sadder, her mouth tireder, the skin on her neck looser; she was basically a worn-down replica of the anxious mother who had seen Horny and me off. She brought me into the living room. There I was somewhat thrown by seeing Arthur sitting up on a chaise longue in a dressing gown. He was recovering from a bout of pneumonia, which explained his absence from the shop. He had aged differently from his wife. His black hair was very thin, and every sinew in his body seemed to stand out. Not feebly, however—angrily. For all the scuffling I'd done, and despite the fact that he was indisposed, I still wouldn't have wanted to cross him. He'd barely been nineteen when Horny was born and was not yet forty-six. He claimed to have paid for his marriage licence by winning a boxing prize. But it had always been as much his disposition as his physique that intimidated me. I only recall seeing him smile once.

One time when I went over to the house, Horny and I had been scrapping, and his nose was bloody. That was when Arthur Ingersoll treated me best. He grinned; he chuckled. When the nose started gushing afresh, Arthur Ingersoll guffawed. He liked it that I'd hit his son. "Do him good. Toughen him up." It ruined my appetite for fights for a whole week.

Today, he didn't come close to smiling. A pout I had sometimes seen cross his pinched features seemed by now to have taken up permanent residence. At least, it never left him all the time I was in his home. It was embarrassing, really, to see such a childish expression on a man his age.

"It's Paul, Arthur," Gladys told him. "Horner's friend, remember?"

"Good afternoon, sir." I didn't think he was going to answer me, so I turned back to Gladys. "It's good to see you both."

"You enlisted in the infantry," Arthur said abruptly. "You ever manage to get transferred to Horny's battery?"

"I wish you wouldn't call him that," Gladys sighed.

"No, Mr. Ingersoll, I didn't." I didn't try to refute the assumption that it would, of course, have been my highest ambition to be promoted from the unworthy service that had been willing to take charge of my sorry carcass to Horny's side at the guns.

"Then he can't tell us anything about Horny's death," Arthur told his wife in a definitive, high-pitched voice.

"Oh, Paul, I hope you can," said Gladys. "We got an official announcement about Horner's dying 'from wounds', and then later his officer wrote. Let me get the letter. It's just here."

She went to her desk in a corner of the room. While she was looking, I noticed a popular book on how to increase your sales on the table at Arthur's elbow, and in the folds of his coverlet one on how to invest your savings. The letter Gladys at length produced was limp from many foldings and unfoldings over the previous four years.

"Dear Mr. and Mrs. Ingersoll," she read. *"You have asked me if I can provide any more details regarding the death of your son than can be gleaned from the official notice. I was not present personally when he died, but understand that he was steadfastly manning the guns under heavy anti-battery fire. A piece of shrapnel hit him in the stomach and, despite prompt action by the stretcher-bearers, he died at the dressing station within the half-hour. I believe he was not conscious during this interval and suffered very little. His wound was of such severity that no surgical skill in the world could have*

saved him. Let me say how sorry I am for your loss, which is also that of his unit and of his country. I can only add that Horner Ingersoll died bravely in the defence of western civilization against barbarous aggression. I give you my word that we who are left will show your son's butchers no mercy. Horner Ingersoll will be avenged. Sincerely, Geoffrey Dundas, Lieutenant, Canadian Field Artillery. That's all he says. Can you add anything, Paul?"

"As a matter of fact—"

"He wasn't there, Gladys," Arthur piped up. "He was infantry. In the trenches. The guns are set up somewhere else entirely. Anyway, what more would you want to know? It's all there in black and white."

"Paul was Horner's friend. I just thought he might have heard something...something more."

"It's all perfectly straightforward. The gunners did their job. The infantry did their job." Arthur nodded towards me, as representing a necessary if inferior branch of the military. I thought it was big of him. "And then," he went on, "the politicians made a lenient peace. The Hun got away with his aggression and is bound to try it again. How Horny died is clear. That he has not, despite what the officer says, been avenged is also clear. Now, can I have my tea?"

I went to the kitchen with Gladys rather than sit with Arthur. She said the other Ingersoll children were well and pursuing the studies Arthur had wished for them. The boy was to be a lawyer; the girl was taking a degree in household science. The family was not suffering financially. They had even bought a small apartment block in the neighbourhood and had four suites to rent out to carefully chosen tenants.

"It's just Horner," Gladys told me.

"It must be dreadful to lose a child," I said lamely.

"Yes, but it's not just that. I feel uneasy about him somehow, as if he wants to tell me something more. You'll think me superstitious."

"No—I—there is—"

"Maybe it's because we've no grave to go to. Is there a grave—over there?"

"Yes," I said. "Yes, of course. With a headstone, in a well-tended cemetery."

"I'd so like to see it."

"I hope you do."

I said I wouldn't stay for tea and asked her to make my excuses to her husband.

Chapter Eleven

Five o'clock on the morning of April 21, 1926 found me walking Toronto's waterfront and contemplating stowing away on a lake freighter. I had still not phoned the inspector. Much as I'd learned about the case since last speaking to him, there was nothing I wanted to say. Ivan MacAllister and Robert "Tinker" Taylor both should have been named as suspects in Digby Watt's murder, but to do so would have seemed to me a sellout of fellow soldiers. Now I was afraid Sam Godwin would turn out to be the third survivor of that bad shell before Ypres, the Sam who that day had spoken—in a roundabout way—of castrating Digby Watt.

Nor did I care to reveal the new dirt on Olive, that she too seemed to have a motive going back to the war and to Digby Watt's profitable manufacture of shells.

Then again, I didn't believe I could excuse myself from the case without having to face Sanderson's awkward questions. I'd wanted to be a detective in order to make my corner of the world a little fairer, but in this case I had to see justice on the side of the vigilantes. Patience in adversity, Edith said, was the theme of the little book Digby had taken to carrying. I couldn't see that he had known much in the way of adversity—not until getting shot. Perhaps he'd been praying his victims be sent patience so they wouldn't rise up against him.

The more I learned about Digby Watt the less I wanted

anybody punished for his murder. This could not be explained. Better to disappear.

Not on the water, however. I remembered why, twelve years before, I'd joined the infantry rather than the navy. It wasn't the fear of drowning. You could drown in a trench. But on land—wet or dry—you were never far from women. Leave might be granted and could sometimes be earned. And, if not, a wound of the right sort could bring you within hours into the company of pretty nurses. I'd soon learned not to wish lightly for wounds, too many of which were of the wrong sort altogether, but the only ship I ever pined for was the troop ship that would bring me home.

I caught the first streetcar of the morning back to my apartment, where a bath, a shave, a pot of coffee and a change of clothes gave me as much new hope as I could expect without a drink. It was certainly a day to be alert. I stowed my flask in a dresser drawer before I left for the house on Linsmore Crescent.

It was still early, and Digby Watt's onetime sweetheart had not yet left for work. She and her aunt—introduced to me as Amelia Prentis—expressed alarm at my early unannounced appearance, but I assured them I simply had some follow-up questions. Mrs. Prentis, still in her housecoat, left the living room to me and her niece. Olive wore a green dress even dingier in tone than her brown one and sported no corsage. Her initial manner was suspicious but less distant than yesterday. Otherwise, she looked as I recalled her. We seated ourselves as before, she on the chesterfield, I in the wing chair nearest the hall. It didn't occur to me either time that this meant turning my back to the door.

"Miss Teddington," I began, "did you have a sister that worked for Peerless Armaments in Hamilton?"

She blinked and swallowed hard. I saw the grief that had

been altogether absent the day before when we had been discussing Digby Watt.

"Yes. I did."

"And did she die as a result of that work?"

Olive nodded.

"Tell me about it."

Olive bit her lip and looked down at her hands where they lay knotted in her lap.

"Did something explode at the plant?"

"No. Oh, no, it was no factory accident. She knew a girl that lost a finger when a fuse went off, and another who got her hair caught and pulled out in a lathe, but Janet..."

"Not an accident. Murder then?"

She wiped her eyes with the backs of her hands.

"Savagery, at least. No policeman wanted to hear—not at the time." Tears continued to mist Olive's eyes, while a cruel little smile tugged up the corners of her lips. "Funny, isn't it?"

This healthy young woman's self-righteousness was beginning to grate on me. No, I hadn't had a sibling die, and I respected her loss. But when it came to savagery, I could tell her first-hand stories that would send her screaming from the room with her hands over her ears.

"I'm not laughing, Miss Teddington. What was the crime?"

"Rape. Violent rape."

Still a hard word for a young woman to use in mixed company. Now we were getting somewhere.

"At the plant?" I asked.

"On her way home. There were two men, wearing caps pulled low and scarves up around their faces, but Janet knew who they were. The father and son that ran the gas station, one too old to fight in the army, one too young. So they used to say. They had enough fight in them to break my sister's nose."

"And why wouldn't the police take her complaint?"

"All because it was six in the morning she got off work instead of six at night."

I begged her pardon.

"Girls on the night shift had to take their chances, the constables said. There was a war on. It was a policy not to report or prosecute attacks on female munitions workers so that recruitment for night work at the plant wouldn't suffer. Digby's plant."

This was a new one on me, but then so many crazy things had been done for the sake of Saving Civilization that I don't know why I was surprised. I imagined myself, a policeman, behind the counter early one morning when this battered and violated young war worker had to be given the cold shoulder. Could I have carried out my instructions? Then I remembered—no need for imagination—myself an infantryman, again in the morning, preparing to go over the top. Never mind the bad shells; had the good shells, the ones that cut the wire to make possible the advance of my platoon—had those shells been bought at such a price?

"I'm sorry," I said. "What happened to her?"

"She had a sweetheart overseas that she had been saving herself for. She couldn't write to him as if nothing had happened. And she couldn't tell him. It would have been hard enough for her to admit what happened, even if the criminals had been brought to justice. Officially, though, there was no crime. Of course, it wasn't till later that I worked this out. I shared a bedroom with her. I was six years younger, barely twelve in 1916 when this happened, so I was told almost nothing at the time. Janet stopped working night shifts. Then, ten weeks later, she was 'in hospital'. Then she was dead. All my mother would say was that an operation had gone wrong. We weren't to speak of it, to anyone, ever."

Olive's voice, while it wobbled a bit, stayed on the rails.

"What happened to her assailants?" I asked.

"The boy joined up and was killed. I think at Passchendaele. The father, last I heard, still runs Billings and Son in the north end. My family left the neighbourhood."

"If you could snap your fingers," I said, "and make Billings disappear from the face of the earth, would you do it?"

She looked at me as if I'd lost my mind. Then her features settled thoughtfully.

"The thing is," she said at last, "I never could snap my fingers." Her right thumb moved noiselessly over her right middle finger.

"That's good enough," I said, snapping my own fingers. "I would."

"I don't have to see him. He *has* disappeared—from my life anyway."

"And Digby Watt? Did you want him gone, after what his plant did to Janet?"

"Gone? Out of my sight, yes. Dead, no."

"But you had a reason for wanting him dead."

"I suppose so."

"Then you lied yesterday, Miss Teddington, when you told me you had no reason for wanting him dead."

"These are police tricks. I held him responsible for what happened to Janet. In my shoes, that might be a reason for you to want him dead. But it wasn't a reason for me."

"Did you kill Digby Watt?"

"No."

"Miss Teddington, why did you come to Toronto last fall?"

"To make a new start."

"Were you living with your parents before you came?"

"With one or the other. My parents separated after Janet's death. Neither household has been what you'd call easy to live in."

"Did any member of your family ever speak of settling scores with Janet's killers?"

"No!" Agitation was beginning to raise the pitch of her voice. "They're not like that. They don't think like that."

"Did you come to this city with the intention of finding and confronting Digby Watt?"

"Not at all. Please—I didn't know his name before I met him at the church. I didn't even think of there being a man—a man like Digby—behind Peerless Armaments."

"Try again," I said. "I want the truth."

"I believe Olive has answered your question, sergeant."

Caught out in my first attempt to browbeat the girl. That'd teach me in future to keep my back to the wall.

I turned and saw Aunt Amelia, dressed for work in cream blouse and black jacket and skirt. She was a heavyset woman with a forbidding set of jowls and a flicker of nervous benevolence around the eyes. I didn't know how long she'd been standing in the doorway.

"Come in, Mrs. Prentis," I said, rising.

"I was wondering, sergeant, how much longer you were going to be. Olive and I have to get down to the shop. If you need more time with her, could you perhaps continue the interview there?"

"It shouldn't be long," I said, hastening to offer her my chair while I shifted to a rocker by the electric hearth. "Please join us."

"Well..." Aunt Amelia sat, evidently in two minds about it.

"Mrs. Prentis, can you tell me why Miss Teddington came to live and work with you last fall?"

"I asked her to. With my husband gone, I needed help in the shop."

"Before Miss Teddington's arrival, did you know Digby Watt?"

"No, we didn't move in the same circles."

"What about at church?"

"My aunt and uncle were Anglicans," said Olive. "She only started going to Danforth Avenue United when I came."

The older woman nodded agreement on both counts.

"You had heard of him, though, Mrs. Prentis?"

"Oh, yes. In the papers, on the radio."

"Mrs. Prentis, did you associate Digby Watt in any way with the death of Miss Teddington's older sister Janet?"

Aunt Amelia, who had been sitting on the edge of the wing chair, allowed her shoulders to sag slightly and the chair back to take a little of her weight. Her voice, however, remained clear and definite.

"No," she said.

"You do know what I'm talking about?"

Aunt Amelia blinked anxiously. Olive stared at the carpet.

"Yes," said the aunt at last. "I know the story, but I never held Digby Watt responsible. He didn't want Janet to suffer what she suffered."

Olive looked at her incredulously.

"You knew all along? You knew, Aunt Amelia, before I ever came to live here that Digby Watt owned Peerless Armaments? You knew all the time I was walking out with Digby?"

"Yes, Olive, I knew. But he owned a dozen companies, each with hundreds of employees. He couldn't look after each and every one and make sure none of them came to harm."

"You knew, and you let me go out with him. Why didn't you tell me?"

"Don't upset yourself now, Olive. You know you get easily upset. We won't discuss this now."

"Excuse me, Mrs. Prentis," I intervened, "but I'd like to hear an answer to your niece's question."

"Oh, sergeant, I'm sorry you have to stir up this ancient history. When you think of all the pain my sister's family has been through... That's just what I brought Olive to Toronto to get her away from."

"You just said you asked me here because you needed my help," declared Olive.

"I thought we could help each other. But really, Olive, I wanted what was best for you. I would have been nothing but pleased for you if you had left me in order to marry Digby Watt."

Olive's mouth worked speechlessly.

"And why," I insisted, "did you not tell Miss Teddington about Digby Watt's connection to Janet?"

"In the first place, I did not see a connection. In every business, accidents happen. Things occur which are neither foreseen nor wanted by the proprietor."

"As your employee," said Olive, "I guess I've been warned."

"Olive! When you calm down, you'll see how unjust that is. Why don't you go and lie down? I'll make do on my own this morning."

Olive's eyes narrowed. Without another word, she left the room. Unflinchingly accepting her angry looks, Aunt Amelia watched her go.

"She's a good worker, sergeant, but she's young—young even for her age. She sees the world in very cut and dried terms. To bring up the subject of Peerless Armaments would only have poisoned her mind against Digby—who was, from all one hears, not just a successful man, but a kind and generous one."

"Wasn't it inevitable, Mrs. Prentis, that she'd find out? In fact, it only took an hour with his children."

"I hoped that by the time she found out, she'd be so fond of him that it wouldn't matter, or wouldn't matter so much. We have to keep hoping, sergeant. We have to look to the future, not dwell on the pain of the past, don't you think? Surely the war taught us that, if nothing else."

It's amazing with what assurance people draw the lessons of war.

"All I know," I said, "is that past pain is the bread and butter of a murder investigation."

"Then you must investigate people who live in the past." Amelia Prentis patted her auburn hair, from which all suspicion of grey had been artfully excluded. "I understand that everyone you interview is not a suspect. Truly I do. But still, I find it strange that you should want to question my niece twice in two days. Yes, she broke with Digby, but she would never have killed him."

"Do you have any idea who did?"

"I don't, sergeant."

"Do you or your niece have a gun, Mrs. Prentis?"

"No, why would we?"

"You have a shop. You take in cash, I suppose. You might feel you wanted to protect it."

"This is Toronto, not the wild west. No, I never felt the need. I'm much more likely to lose money by having the shop closed during business hours."

"Have you ever shot a gun?"

"Yes. My father used to take me hunting. He thought it was part of living in this country, so he insisted on teaching all of his children to shoot."

"And grandchildren?"

"That I wouldn't know."

"I didn't see a garage. Do you or your niece have a car?"

"No, sergeant, neither of us drive. My shop is within walking distance, at Danforth and Coxwell."

"I'll make a point of looking in," I said. "The night before last, between one thirty and two thirty a.m., were you and Miss Teddington both home?"

"Yes, certainly. And asleep."

"What time did you last see her that night?"

"It would have been close to ten."

"Could she have gone out after ten without your knowledge?"

"Impossible. I sleep with my bedroom door open, and the head of the stairs is just outside."

Her voice was clear, calm, authoritative. I couldn't help thinking what a credible witness Amelia Prentis would make. A formidable obstacle to any case against Olive.

"Could *you* have gone out without *her* knowledge?" I ventured.

"I could have, but I wouldn't have left her alone at night. Certainly not without telling her. I promised my sister to take care of Olive."

"And did your sister or her husband know Olive was seeing Janet's former employer?"

"I have to go now." She stood up, giving a brisk tug to the bottom of her suit jacket.

"Nevertheless," I said.

"The answer to your question, sergeant, and it is the last one I'll answer, is *no.*"

Chapter Twelve

At the end of Amelia Prentis's street, I picked up the day's *Examiner*. In his latest story, Ivan MacAllister wrote that it now appeared Digby Watt's killing might have a motive going back to the war. Peerless Armaments was named, and the subject of war profits hinted at, but the defective shells were never mentioned. I suspected that the discretion was not all self-imposed, but—however timid or sycophantic his editors—Ivan had managed to raise subtle doubts about Digby Watt's image as a shining knight of the home front.

In view of the terms on which we had parted the day before, I did not expect to find Ivan particularly co-operative, so I decided to start with Tinker. I had no desire to return to the station yet. Taking Digby Watt's exercise book out of my inside jacket pocket, I consulted the Queen Street West address at the head of the murdered man's reply to Tinker Taylor's letter. When I arrived, I saw that it was a rooming house of the sort that caters to a transient population and immediately lowered my expectation of finding Taylor still in residence.

Fate smiled, however. Tinker was in. Not happy to have his door pounded on at nine thirty a.m., but in—as demonstrated by the abuse that answered my knock.

"Go 'way. Jump in the lake."

I knocked louder.

"Go a-way. Knock once more I'll..." A deliberative

mumble. "I'll break every finger on your hand. Joint at a time."

This would have been the moment for me to identify myself as a police detective, but I had a different approach in mind.

"Open up, Tinker. It's Horny's friend, Paul."

"Who?"

"Paul—I helped you carry Horny Ingersoll to the dressing station, remember? Second Ypres, 1915."

"Bugger you. I don't know you."

The voice was deep and ringing. I remembered Tinker as a big, full-muscled man—in 1915 a prime candidate for anchor on a tug-of-war team. Possibly seedier now, but still likely to be a handful. Might it not be wiser to go to the landlord, show some identification, get a key?

"Mr. Peerless is dead, Tinker. I've come to let you buy me a drink. Mr. Peerless Armaments—Digby Watt. The man whose bad shells killed Horny Ingersoll and who knows how many more. Remember you asked me if I wouldn't like to get the guy, the guy who made those shells, in a dark alley? Someone did, Tinker. Someone got him in a dark alley and let him have it. Come drink with me, Tinker—or have you forgotten your pals?"

I heard steps approach the door from the other side. I stepped smartly back, but not smartly enough. The door flew open. An enormous fist gathered up my jacket lapels, shirt front, and tie and yanked me into Tinker's room. Once inside, I still couldn't see much of the premises. Tinker's chest, bursting through a soiled pyjama top, and Tinker's angry unshaved face took up my whole field of vision. He pinned me against a wall with his right hand while with his left he slammed my head repeatedly back against the plaster.

"Who's forgotten [slam] his pals? [slam] Who?"

I scarcely thought this the best posture for fruitful talk, so I brought one metal-plated heel down smartly on Tinker's bare right foot and at the same time got hold of one of those places on Tinker's neck where a little pressure goes a long way. The tussle soon ended. Tinker had a strong man's reckless arrogance and a gunner's lack of experience with hand-to-hand combat. I stuck my right leg out as a fulcrum and toppled him over it.

As the big man was going down, his hand swung out and caught the handle of a dresser drawer; out it flew, flinging its contents over the already untidy room.

"You fight like a poof." Tinker pulled himself to a sitting position and rubbed his toes. "Hope you're planning to fix that crack in my wall. Ruins the day-core."

Meaning apparently the crack my skull had made while Tinker was using it as a hammer. I judged the crack went well enough with the torn blind, the cigarette burns on the few sticks of furniture, the bulbless lamps, and the carpet littered with clothes and newspapers.

And, from the dislodged drawer, two German nudist magazines.

I picked one up and riffled the pages. A novelty, certainly, but not exactly racy, even if it was still impossible to buy the like openly in Canada. But then, stored between two pages of young men thinking pure thoughts and striking athletic poses, something different caught my eye. A sepia photograph of a standing male nude, in profile and backlit to make the most of his state of arousal. The model's face was coyly turned away from the camera, but I didn't have to look far to guess his identity.

Tinker hobbled to a seat on the edge of his bed, wiped his nose on his pyjama collar and tested his neck to see if it still swivelled through its full normal range.

"Hey, put that down!" he burst out. "Who the sod are you anyway?"

"I know you artillerymen are all deaf, Tinker, but if you watch my lips this time you should be able to get it."

I proceeded to recount with every detail I could remember my visit to Tinker's battery, the death of Horner Ingersoll, and the talk I had had afterwards with Tinker, Ivan and Sam.

Tinker scratched his stubbled chin. His thick chocolate-brown moustache was badly trimmed, and his thin brown hair looked as if he'd cut it himself. Without a mirror. His face otherwise was unremarkable. The best that could be said of it was that his dark eyes were starting to focus.

"You're Paul," Tinker declared, as if this were a vital piece of information I had been holding back. "You went to school with Horny Ingersoll."

"Yes, and the man that killed him is dead."

"You're late," said Tinker. "I heard yesterday. I've already been celebrating."

"No harm celebrating twice. What I had in mind was gathering together everyone that was there that day. You, me, Ivan—he's a newspaperman, as you may know—and Sam. Only I've no idea how to get in touch with Sam."

"Prayer," said Tinker.

"You'd know his last name at least."

"Rossi. But it won't do you any good."

"Oh." I had been slow on the uptake, because I wasn't expecting to hear sense from Tinker's mouth. "You mean I'll find it on a headstone in Europe."

"Killed by anti-battery fire two years later. At least it was Fritz that got him and not some war profiteer."

"Shame all the same."

I took a moment to remember Sam's finely chiselled

features and cool, prompt action in getting Horny onto the improvised stretcher.

"Tinker," I said at last, "you didn't plug Digby Watt yourself, did you?"

"With a little squirt of a gun like that? Must have been a little man did it, or a girl. Was it you?"

"What gun *do* you keep?"

"I don't, but I can get one if I feel hounded. How did you find me anyway?"

"I don't know if you know this, Tinker, but Mr. Peerless had a summer place up north. I had a look in there the other night. A desk got broken open, and guess what I found. *Dear Mr. Peerless... I haven't had much good fortune since the war, while you dirty profiteers have just gone on making one fortune after another... Worst wishes...* Did you ever get an answer?"

"Turd like that? Not a chance." Tinker dropped his pyjama bottoms and started poking through a pile of discarded briefs in a corner of the room, sniffing and tossing each aside, then at last easing himself into the first pair. "So you're a housebreaker now, Paul? You don't look like it."

"I can't say *you* look much like your portrait." Tinker in the nude photo had his hair professionally barbared, for one thing, and his feet planted for strutting rather than shambling.

"Have you thought maybe you don't excite me? Give me that."

I didn't, though. Tinker had broken wind, and I was using the stiff rectangle of photo paper as a fan.

"That must have burned you," I pursued. "After spilling the secrets of your soul to old Digby, giving him a chance to say sorry, at least, and maybe try to make some amends, you get nothing. You must have hated him worse than before."

"You really want me to say I bumped him off, don't you? The blinking letter wasn't even my idea. I was in a bad way last summer. No work. No prospects. Ivan put me up to writing Peerless, even helped me with the words. I'm better with piano keys."

Here was unexpected news. I tried to picture the hearing-damaged gorilla of a gunner hunched over a keyboard.

"So you are in touch with Ivan."

"Not what you'd call close contact."

"He take this?"

"Heck no. Cripes! What are you talking about?"

"I just meant the picture."

"Oh. Give it here then, and let me look."

"He has a real way with a camera, does Ivan." I surrendered the photo.

Tinker was glad to get it back in his possession and flattered as well.

"You think so?" he asked.

"We all have our talents. Where do you play piano?"

"At the movies. The Alhambra took me on in September when everyone came back to the city from summer holidays. It's regular work—except I took last night off." Tinker was dressed now, in a moth-eaten turtleneck, a surprisingly new and well-cut pair of grey flannels, and scuffed work boots. "Let's get some coffee, copper."

"What are you calling me that for?"

Tinker gave me a punch on the arm that teetered on the borderline between friendly and sadistic.

"Don't judge a man's smarts by what he shows when he wakes up too soon after drinking too much."

"I'd like you to tell that to my inspector." I thought my laugh sounded forced. "So just where were you between one thirty and two thirty night before last?"

"That's a bad time for alibis. Whose company were *you* keeping, Paul?"

"Don't change the subject."

"See what I mean?" Tinker guffawed. "Even when someone could swear you had no opportunity to be shooting down profiteers in the street, you might not want it known who you slept with."

Try as I might, and I ended up buying him toast as well as coffee, I could get no more out of him.

Chapter Thirteen

"You didn't report last night, Paul. I'm docking you a day's pay."

"You wanted me to call before I went to bed, sir. I haven't actually been to bed yet."

"Two days' pay for arguing jesuitically. You were seen with a bottle of Aspirin in the washroom just now. Do you have another headache?"

"It doesn't ache in that way. I bumped it."

"You were drinking last night, Paul, weren't you? God's truth now."

"A little, but I didn't enjoy it."

The inspector lit another match and set it to the contents of his favourite meerschaum. He was smoking a mixture that smelled like roofing tar and not appearing to enjoy it much either.

I was sitting in his cramped office with the door closed. No other cops were present. I'd noticed that Sanderson's way with investigations was to keep the strings in his own hands: the men he assigned to particular aspects of a case reported to him individually rather than assemble as a group. He'd plead lack of meeting space at HQ. He'd pay lip service to teamwork. All the same, you can bet it suited him to have the spokes that were his detectives communicate mainly through the inspectorial hub. Will to power? Absolutely. But he also had to soften and blur the professional jealousies bound to arise among so many underlings of equal rank. Only by operating as he did could he have given me so much to do. I should have thanked him. Under most circumstances, I liked paddling my own canoe. The deuce of it was that the big job he was thrusting on me—to finger someone for Watt's murder—was the one job I didn't want.

"So, Paul," he said, "whom do we arrest?"

"Sir, I'd like to be taken off this case."

Sanderson gave me his hellfire glare.

"Why?"

"This is painful for me to talk about," I said, "so I hope you won't press me for details. It's my mother out in Cape Breton. Her angina is troubling her again, and the doctor has cabled to say she could go any time. I should be at her bedside."

"You have no mother, man. You've never had a mother, and if you ever had had one, she'd never have set so much as a big toe in Cape Breton. Pull yourself together."

I ignored this mark of disrespect and soldiered on—

"My brother would go, but he's trying to set a new flagpole-sitting record—and my sister's no good in a sick room, not since she sprained her wrist playing mah-jong."

"One of your few virtues as a subordinate, Paul, is that you have no family, no family emergencies, no excuses. Ever."

"I'd still like to be assigned other work. The truth is I've no sympathy with the murdered man."

"Good. I wouldn't want sentiment clouding your judgement. Your job isn't to sympathize; it's to deliver to the Crown an accused and enough evidence to secure a guilty verdict."

"You have more than twenty other detective sergeants, sir."

"Good men all of them—most of them. But I assigned you to the Watt murder, and there you'll stay. Request denied."

"But—"

"Sergeant! The subject is *closed.*"

I took a deep breath of well-used pipe smoke and went back to work.

"Last night, I brought in Watt's Remington Autoloading rifle. Has the university made anything of it?"

"As a matter of fact, I was just reading the analyst's report when you came in. Professor Linacre did some tests on it. What's more, the two bullets have been recovered from Digby Watt's body. They both ran into bones and are to a degree misshapen; that'll make it difficult to link them with confidence to a specific gun. However, they aren't Remington rounds. Linacre has identified them as Automatic Colt Pistol ammunition, which cannot be fired from Watt's rifle."

"Here's a handgun I'd like them to look at." I passed it across Sanderson's desk. I had already removed the three bullets from the magazine, dumping them into an envelope without touching them—in case I wanted them dusted for fingerprints later. "I found it in the dockyard area."

"You'll have to be more specific than that if the lab is to spend time on it. Is it a Colt?"

It wasn't often I caught the inspector out, and I could only wish I felt more like gloating.

"No, sir, but there are easily a hundred different makes of pistol that fire .25 ACP."

"Own goal," Sanderson huffed. "Linacre can't go testing hundreds of guns, whether there's any plausible connection to Watt's murder or not."

"I'm not sure that there's a connection, but I'd like it tested."

"Where did you find it? It wasn't just lying on the street,

was it? I suppose it was at the bootlegger's."

"Let's say it was at the bootlegger's, and Digby Watt was a temperance advocate. Is that connection enough?"

"Who is this bootlegger?"

I didn't answer.

"Well," said Sanderson, "we're conducting a murder investigation here, and we don't want to get sidetracked. You can always tell me later." He tucked the pistol in a drawer. "Now about that strike leader Sam Godwin..."

"I haven't tracked him down yet," I said. I was feeling keener to do so now that I knew it wasn't the Sam from Horny's battery.

"Cruickshank has. Our Bolshie union organizer is disturbing the peace of Winnipeg with public meetings, and scores of witnesses attest he was a thousand miles from Bay and Adelaide the night before last. Do you have anything more promising on the political angle—as opposed to the personal?"

"Sometimes the two intersect, sir."

I told the inspector about Olive's blaming Digby Watt for the death of her sister Janet. Sanderson expressed no surprise that the police had been ordered to ignore assault allegations made by women working night shifts.

"How tight is Miss Teddington's alibi?" was all he said.

"Her aunt, Amelia Prentis, denies Olive could have been out of her house at any time it was possible for the murder to have been committed."

"Do you suspect a conspiracy, Paul?"

This was the second time Sanderson had clutched at this straw, but my bias was for a simple solution. Multiple accused made for a messier trial.

"The aunt denies sharing Olive's view of Watt's guilt. She sounds sincere."

"Still, family is family, and when your niece is in trouble, you may lie to save her even if you don't agree with her."

"I'll see if either woman has a vehicle registered in her name. The aunt claims not. I'll also have the taxi companies review their records. There would have been no streetcars or buses at the time of the murder, and it's a two-hour walk from their house."

"Do whatever wraps this up. Speaking of records, Knight did some digging on that rum-running case. Curtis Ritter got a light sentence for testifying against his gang. But he was carrying a Mauser ten-shot magazine pistol when arrested, more firepower than anyone on our force has access to. This is the joker who told you he never used guns!"

"I'll speak to him again."

"Speak? Speak nothing. An arrest is what I need, Paul—by tomorrow night. An arrest that will stick. Get to it."

Back at my desk, I made phone calls and collected information without much expectation of wrapping up the case. There had never been a driving permit issued to Olive Teddington, Amelia Prentis, or Amelia Bowen—as I discovered she had been called before marriage—although of course the aunt was old enough to have been driving since before permits were required. Neither had a car registered in her name. No taxi trips had been made from the immediate vicinity of either Amelia Prentis's house or shop to that of Digby Watt's office on the night of April 19/20—although of course Olive or Amelia or both could have walked at least part way at either end of the trip.

I wondered if getting a conviction were indeed all the inspector cared about. Would he send an innocent man or woman to the gallows just to get rid of the pressure a celebrity murder put him under? I had been a policeman eight years now in total, from 1911 to 1913 and 1920 on.

I'd been a detective sergeant for two years, three months. Sanderson had been there all along. He had shown me some indulgence these past two days, but was no softie. With no facetious intent, he would say that if an accused were wrongly convicted of one crime, the blighter was doubtless guilty of something worse.

While crude at the best of times, this maxim seemed to me particularly inapplicable to the present case. If, for example, Morris Watt had lost patience with his controlling father and blasted away at him one dark night, it would likely have been the first violent act of his life. And if he were sentenced to hang for patricide and were innocent, one could scarcely fall back on the comforting assumption that he had previously got away with another crime equal or greater. The same went for Olive, or Lavinia or Edith. The only jail-bird in the picture was Curtis. The only known one, at least.

I proceeded to check whether either Tinker Taylor or Ivan MacAllister had criminal records. Ivan, I learned, had once been suspected of tampering with a crime scene before the arrival of police, but nothing had been proved, and he had also provided clues leading to convictions, so the balance of police opinion was in his favour. Tinker, by contrast, had convictions and a few days' lock-up time to his discredit. Drunk and disorderly—naturally. Bad debts—owed principally to landlords. Committing a public nuisance—urinating against the doors of Massey Hall. I rather liked that one: had they offended the cinema Paderewski by not inviting him to give a concert there? A year ago, Tinker had been arraigned for sodomy and acquitted. Nothing, however, indicated any involvement with firearms in the seven years since his discharge from the army.

So, back to Curtis. I called the fingerprint expert at

Station Number One. He was still going over the Gray-Dort, but had so far found no loops or whorls anywhere near the steering linkage. I wasn't holding my breath. Meanwhile, there was a note from Detective Sergeant Howarth regarding Stone's Garage. The place seemed reputable to him, and they backed Curtis all the way. So the only thing I had on the chauffeur was that he had been less than forthcoming about the Mauser. If he could handle that much heat, he'd have no trouble with the smaller pistol that had killed Digby. I phoned the Watt residence. Nita told me that Curtis and Miss Watt were out in the Austin and not expected till six o'clock.

Still four hours away.

I tried not to think of the hollow space that was crying out to be filled by an ounce and a half of rye. It wasn't easy to say where exactly in my anatomy this craving was located. My mouth was dry, but that wasn't it. Not the throat either. Further down, in the chest. Where the heart should be, and maybe was. My heart's desire was Seagram's whisky. I hadn't even the decency to be ashamed. So often you're wrong about what you want. What you plan and work for, what you believe will make your heart rejoice, may not even touch the tickle. Drink always made you want more drink, true, but it definitely did its job. There was nothing else that gave so reliably. You dropped your coin in the vending machine and out popped the prize. Every time.

Drink and not enjoy it? The idea was ludicrous.

But I was not going to have a drink. Just steps from City Hall, at 90 Queen Street West, there was a place called Uneeda Lunch. I took the hint.

After a two-sandwich blowout, I went back to Sanderson's office. The inspector wasn't in, but his centre desk drawer was unlocked. I removed and pocketed the pistol I had asked him to send for tests. I took the Harley-Davidson round to Cliff Braddock's to get it patched with something more substantial than chewing gum and whisked myself up to the U. of T.

Professor Dalton Linacre should have been lodged in the Chemistry Building, since that was his department, but overcrowding had resulted in his office and lab being wedged into one twenty by twenty-two foot room in the bowels of the Mining Building on College Street. I'd been there on occasion to drop off anything from safe-crackers' jimmies to specimens of deceased parties' vomit, and—whether the analysis required was toxicological, metallurgical or something in between—Linacre always fired back a report within thirty-six hours. And we weren't the only constabulary bringing him these brainteasers. His mail bag must have been full of them, for his responsibilities were province-wide. Small wonder he never seemed to have much time for chat. I don't know when he had time to give his lectures, let alone sleep.

Linacre's door, like all the others on the brick corridor, sported a huge pane of ripple glass. A stack of horizontal stripes that might have been a person didn't move when I knocked, but I was told to come in, so I did. A plank and two-by-four partition subdivided the room. I was now standing in the smaller portion, evidently the office as opposed to the laboratory.

Linacre was hunched over a pharmacopoeia and a pile of notes at a cramped desk facing the side wall. His wavy black hair was parted low on the left and tufted up a little at the back, where it likely didn't show in the mirror. He wore wire-rim spectacles, a black toothbrush moustache and a smart bottle-green bow tie. That he was no upstart was evident from the condition of his lab coat, which was as limp and discoloured as noodles stewed in dishwater. I thought he might be five years older than I, approaching forty.

He looked around and, whether from memory or trained observation, recognized me as a policeman.

"Just leave it on the table, whatever it is," he said. "Has your inspector told me what I'm to do with it?"

There was no surface space available on any table I could see.

"Detective Sergeant Paul Shenstone," I said, hoping he'd overlook the part about needing authorization from the inspector. "I'm investigating the Digby Watt shooting."

"Three .25 ACP bullets, one with its nose in a book, two knocked about by deceased's rib cage. You haven't brought me the cartridge cases by any chance?"

"Be nice, wouldn't it?" I said. "Could this have been the murder weapon?"

Linacre lifted his spectacles onto the top of his head and peered at the little semi-automatic I handed him. He slid out the magazine.

"I'll show you the best we can do. First, I'll get you to fire off a few rounds. No marksmanship required."

"You're spoiling the fun," I said.

The professor went to a vast grey metal cabinet with hundreds of small drawers and found in one of them bullets as similar as possible to those removed from Watt's body. He tried to match not just make and type but date of manufacture. Apparently satisfied, he charged the clip and slid it back into the pocket pistol. Then he unlocked the door in the floor-to-ceiling partition and led me into the lab portion of his workspace.

"Had to build this wall to keep the crime stuff secret," he grumbled. "Obscure glass in the windows as well. Damned nuisance. Now, this long metal box you see is packed with cotton wool and sectioned off by light wooden partitions so I can find the slugs after you fire them off."

I liked the way his voice brightened up as soon as he started talking about his work. I did not like the thought of firing the piece of junk I'd taken from May. Still, it would be a greater disaster for the forces of law and order in Ontario if Linacre's hand were to be blown off than if I lost mine. I took up a shooter's stance at the end of the box and waited for his signal.

"What are you waiting for?" was the form in which he gave it. "Christmas?"

The small room, even with sound-proofing panels, made the reports loud. I emptied the gun without mishap and found the experience rather like shooting into space. Into an indifferent universe. There was no body to be seen crumpling as you looked down the sights, not even a distant target blossoming with tightly grouped perforations. All your sound and fury for nothing.

As I fired, the gun threw the empty cartridge cases diagonally out to my right and back against the wall, from which they bounced harmlessly. Linacre scooped them up. It took him longer to recover the bullets from his box contraption. When two of the six were back in his possession, he led me to what he called a comparison microscope. From this point, I was very much at sea. I simply couldn't get my eyes to pick out the rifling grooves on the projectiles, or rather I saw them without sufficient comprehension to make them speak to me. I had to rely on Linacre, and Linacre could not be definitive. The most that could be concluded was that the bullets recovered from the deceased were consistent with those fired from May's gun. If this was not the murder weapon, then a similar model likely was.

When I thanked him, he told me to find the missing cartridge cases. Unlike the bullets extracted from Watt, they would not be misshapen, and a comparison with those cases he had collected today would settle the question whether this Spanish Prince was the murder weapon. It sounded as if he loved guns, but maybe he just loved puzzles.

"Easier said than done," I muttered.

"Don't worry if it takes a while," said the scientist. "I've enough work to keep me here till eleven tonight at least."

When I closed Linacre's door behind me and found myself once more in the brick corridor of the Mining Building basement, I felt like slugging somebody. The fight at the blind pig last night and my roughhousing with Tinker had just whetted my appetite. But there was new venom to it too. I was angry with my assignment to pin this murder on someone. I wondered if I could make myself mean and angry enough to do it. A group of students passed me on my way out to the street. I nodded pleasantly and guess I managed pretty well not to look like a killer.

A phone message from Edith was waiting for me at HQ. She wanted to know if the Gray-Dort could be returned in time for the funeral on the twenty-fourth. The number she left was that of the Watt residence on Glen Road, so possibly she and Curtis were now home.

Instead of returning her call, I rode over. This time I didn't stop to be announced at the front door, and when I swung the old motorcycle smartly around the corner of the drive to the garage, I surprised Nita and Curtis in a close embrace. The girl was on tiptoes with her lips pressed up against her man's, her arms locked around his chest. His square head inclining to the right, he eagerly returned her kiss while holding and caressing her waist.

Hot stuff, I thought, but what interested me more was

the way they sprang apart on hearing my Harley-Davidson. Curtis, a precise man in my experience, seemed to stumble and to favour an uncommonly stiff right foot. Nita reached for him solicitously and was pushed away.

Back in possession of himself, Curtis was striding forward with a decidedly dirty look by the time I had dismounted and propped my machine on its stand.

"You lied to me, Curtis," I said, not waiting for words to go with the look. "Would you excuse us a moment, Nita?"

The housemaid, who had rushed forward, put her hand to her mouth, looking from one of us to the other.

"Go in the house," said Curtis.

When she had done so, I returned to the attack.

"You were stupid enough to tell me you never used firearms. All the time knowing exactly what I'd find when I read the arrest report."

"I didn't use it. Look, you don't have the right—"

"A Mauser automatic. Just for show?"

"They made me carry it. For emergencies, they said."

"But you'd have shot policemen with it. Don't pretend you wouldn't."

"I wouldn't. Ah, what does it matter?"

"It matters, Curtis. It matters because you stand to gain handsomely from your employer's death—so handsomely that you fancied your legacy combined with Nita's would console her for marrying without her parents' blessing. It matters because you would have known better than anyone how to sabotage the Gray-Dort. Most of all, it matters because you are the only person connected with Digby Watt in the habit of carrying a pistol."

"I never shot it. I couldn't have shot it."

"Hooey. You were in the war: you know all about guns. Pull down your right sock."

Curtis didn't move.

"Your foot is wood, isn't it? Nita as much as told me you'd been shot in the war, but I didn't think anything of it until I saw you stumble just now. If you want to keep your secret, you'll have to be less embarrassed about kissing. She's a terrific kid, nothing to be ashamed of. I just hope she's not a hanged man's widow before she gets to be a wife."

"Easy to pick on the servants, isn't it?" The effort at self-control had turned Curtis's face very purple.

"I'm more on your side than you think," I said. I didn't want to goad him into apoplexy. "I've nothing in common with your employers."

The chauffeur snorted.

"Sure, Curtis. You and I were both soldiers. We should be able to understand each other. You don't waste words. I respect that. And yet you were very clever last night the way you let it be dragged out of you that Olive Teddington accused Digby Watt of killing her sister. That was an excellent way of diverting suspicion from yourself. Of course Olive never said that at all, but you were very convincing."

"She did."

"It's no good, Curtis. I have the gun you used. Here it is. Packs less punch than that Big Bertha you're used to, but it's so much easier to hide." I showed him the Spanish pocket pistol and then made it disappear completely inside my fist. "Easier to hide, easier to get rid of. And deadly enough when your victim trusts you, lets you in close." With the hand that held the gun, I tapped the region on Curtis's chest corresponding to that where the bullets had entered his employer's. "You're the *last* person Digby Watt should have trusted, aren't you? And the last person he did trust."

"It's a frame," said Curtis, his voice loud with consternation. "I'm not answering any more questions."

"You'll answer here or at the station. Do you want Nita to see you go in handcuffs?"

"I won't speak without a lawyer."

"Oh, does the accused have the right to a lawyer in Germany? I didn't know. It was in the German army you fought, wasn't it? *Nicht wahr,* Kurt Ritter?"

A vein in Curtis's temple was throbbing; he was within an inch of hitting me. Then I would really have some leverage over him. Already within arm's length, I moved in even closer to make it more tempting for Curtis to lay hands on me.

"Actually, sergeant, he was born in Kitchener, Ontario, and served in France as a stretcher bearer with the 9th Canadian Field Ambulance." Morris Watt had emerged from the house, a pained look on his handsome face. "I'll be glad to arrange legal representation for Curtis. In the meantime, if you have no warrant for his arrest and don't have to rush off, the family would appreciate a word with you in the living room."

Chapter Fourteen

The Watts' living room was large, tidy and drably papered in blue-grey. Nothing was worn out, nothing brand new. A buffet-sized Zenith radio with five knobs, two dials and two ample battery-storage compartments was the most conspicuous item of furniture—even though the Heintzman grand piano soaked up more of the surplus floor space. You'd never guess the Watts' means from the pictures on the walls, all of which were mass-produced colour prints. All, that is, except for one winter scene in oils. I thought I recognized the original of an advertisement for Canada Ski and Snowshoe. Without the printing, of course.

The family had evidently been enjoying a before-dinner drink. Lemonade. Morris poured me a glass from a crystal pitcher and with determined civility indicated a blue-grey armchair. It had more padding than the furniture down at the office. I didn't mind it at all.

"Good afternoon, Mrs. Watt. Miss Watt. I'm afraid I can't promise you your car back in time for the funeral."

Lavinia appeared attached to a divan at several points. A crossword puzzle book and gold mechanical pencil lay on the end table beside her. Her dress today was pearl grey and tasteful, though perhaps a little voguishly short for the room. She gave me a smile that was warmer than a formality—non-committal, yet communicative of the hospitality she would have offered me if it had not been too much effort for her to move.

"Never mind, Mr. Shenstone," she said. "I'm sure we can make other arrangements."

"Morris already has," said Edith, perched on the edge of her chair. "There's something much more important we wanted to speak to you about."

Her dress also was short—black and low in the waist, with a starkly white collar. Last evening I had at no time seen her in strong light and had somehow forgotten what an incredibly vivid picture she made. Glowing white skin, piercing blue eyes, hair that—under the incandescent bulbs of the electrolier—made brilliant black no contradiction in terms. I didn't know if there were any causal connection between an immaculately shaped mouth and a clear voice, but I perceived they sorted well and in combination lent anything said, wise or otherwise, a dangerous plausibility.

"Yes?" I hadn't quite got Curtis off my mind yet, but recognized that the interruption was no more than might have been expected. I should have taken the chauffeur to the station right away. "I'm all yours."

"My sister," said Morris, "tells me there is new evidence as to a motive for killing our father."

"Go ahead, Mr. Watt."

Morris and Edith sat to either side of Lavinia's divan. Plainly Edith wanted to speak and Morris did not, but as he had been addressed he took up the charge, and Edith held her peace.

"Last night you found an allegation that Peerless Armaments made defective shells during the war." Morris cleared his throat. "I have now spoken by phone to men who worked at the Hamilton plant at the time, and I've found that allegation to be true. The case of the gunner whose letter you have, sergeant, is not an isolated one.

Between twelve and sixteen hundred bad shells left the factory. Half of those failed inspection and were never shipped. We've no way of knowing how many of the others blew up on being fired on the Western Front. The Allied gunners who died as a result were of course never reported or recorded separately from the victims of enemy activity. Each of those gunners must have had comrades, like this Mr. Taylor, who blamed Peerless for what they saw as unnecessary deaths. I am told other Canadian arms manufacturers produced bad shells at an equal or worse rate. Our country was pressed to contribute to the war effort in areas where we had little to no expertise. I'm not saying this, however, to minimize the problem at Peerless, which was aggravated by the deception Taylor alludes to. It is possible that a couple of thousand Canadian servicemen came home from Europe with little love for the Peerless name or for whoever was behind it. As I told you, sergeant, I spent the war in England. I had no idea what was happening in Hamilton, and not the foggiest notion of the consequences across the Channel in Europe. I am cut up about this discovery, to put it mildly. How could it have happened? All I can think is that, as a thoroughly honest man himself, my father put too much trust in the integrity of his subordinates. With nightmarish results. Nonetheless, and here is where my opinion differs from my sister's, I do not see how news of the defective shells advances your investigation. On the one hand, it gives you too many suspects. You cannot question two thousand men. On the other, my experience of servicemen leads me to think they are unvindictive. Men who have been hurt as badly as men can be did not come home looking for the blood of those who wronged them. Some may have got into trouble as they struggled to readjust to civilian life, but not the kind of trouble we've been forced to look at since the night before last. *Vendetta* is not an English word."

"You speak," said Edith, "from knowledge of your own forgiving nature. As for vendetta being un-English, may I remind you that the most admired play in the language is about a son who gets in trouble because he neglects the duty of revenge."

"Do you think she means *Hamlet?*" asked Lavinia, perhaps less because she was in any doubt herself than because she tactfully feared I might be out of my depth.

"Shakespeare's world is not ours, Edie," Morris mildly observed.

"Fine. Let's take your two thousand suspects. Fewer than a hundred would live in Toronto, and only one has—to our knowledge—written a letter that closes 'worst wishes'."

"Mr. Watt," I said, "before today, had you ever heard or read of Robert Taylor?"

"I don't believe so. There were always so many people petitioning my father for help of one kind or another, and when he wanted to find work for ex-servicemen he regarded as deserving, he invariably left the arrangements to me. But I've checked my files and found no mention of Taylor."

"Have you spoken to Taylor yet, Mr. Shenstone?" Edith asked.

"I'm not at liberty to say."

"*I* haven't," Edith continued. "He sounded fearsome. But I've done one or two other things. When I read Ivan MacAllister's article this morning, I phoned *him* up and asked whether he knew Taylor."

"I'd prefer these inquiries were left to the police detectives," said Morris.

I nodded full agreement.

"You'll be quoted in tomorrow's edition, Edie," Lavinia warned. "See if you aren't."

"Right at the start, I told him I didn't want my name or anything I said in print. He may flout me, but I say it was worth the risk."

"Did he tell you anything?"

"Yes, Lavinia, he did. He told me he was there before Ypres when that shell blew up."

"The shell Taylor writes of?" asked Morris.

"The very same. He was working the same gun. And he sounds bitter. I think he has as good a motive for shooting Dad as Taylor does. And what's more, it was Ivan MacAllister that found Dad's body."

"Did you know all this, sergeant?" asked Morris.

"Not at liberty to say, I'm afraid."

"You must have to say that often, Mr. Shenstone," Lavinia commiserated. "You should have a short form. Something like NALTS—Not At Liberty To Say."

"My liberty," said Edith, "is not so circumscribed. And uneasy as that liberty may make my brother, I can answer his question. Mr. Shenstone not only knew. He was there as well. He helped carry the fatally wounded man to the dressing station."

Mr. and Mrs. Watt looked questioningly at Edith, then at each other. With what manner of being were they living?

"Mr. Shenstone and this man Taylor and Ivan MacAllister?" said Lavinia. "How extraordinary!"

"All there," Edith assured her. "And a fourth man named Sam Rossi, who was later killed by the Germans."

"You shouldn't believe all you hear from newspapermen," I advised. "As you'll see when you're misquoted tomorrow, Miss Watt, they love a good story."

"Then you'd better just tell us, Mr. Shenstone, as soon

as I say something you know to be false... Nothing yet? Good. Because this family is both grieving the loss of a very remarkable father and trying to make sense of the singularly upsetting and baffling manner of his death. I think we've a right to the truth."

I'd had this from relatives before and knew my lines. I don't think I made them sound too pat.

"A homicide concerns everyone." I paused here to look from Edith to Lavinia to Morris. "It undermines trust right through a society. I respect your grief, but my obligations aren't just to your family. That's why I can't always take you into my confidence to the extent you might wish."

"You must find society an impersonal master," Edith rejoined. "Forgive me for thinking that some of those other obligations you feel are to the man you carried on that stretcher, Horner Ingersoll. Of all his pals present that day, you knew him the longest and the best. Yes, the others had fought at his side, but you were the only one there who had been to school with him."

Lavinia actually sat up.

"How dreadful for you, Mr. Shenstone!" she breathed. "Edie has told us the nature of your friend's wounds."

I bet the ladies had had fun with that.

"Is what Edith says true, sergeant?"

"He doesn't deny it, Morris," Edith observed.

"In that case," said Morris, "while I also sympathize with your loss, I can't think that you are the right man to conduct this investigation."

"Please feel free, sir, to tell that to Inspector Sanderson." I had hoped to be removed from the case without having my involvement reach Sanderson's ears, but Tinker and Ivan were both leaky vessels. I wondered if more beans had been spilled. "Go on, Miss Watt."

"You mean there's more?" asked Lavinia.

"I don't think we need detain the sergeant further." Morris made to rise.

"I'd like him to hear the rest," Edith protested. "Please."

Morris relented.

"Mr. Shenstone was only visiting the battery that day," Edith continued. "He was not a gunner, but rather a non-commissioned officer in an infantry regiment. The 48th Highlanders of Canada, to be exact. That is as much as I could get from Ivan MacAllister, but it was enough to lead me to Mr. Shenstone's war record. Truly, Morris, this is not as boring as your impatient face would suggest."

"Morris doesn't look bored, Edie," Lavinia loyally objected. "He looks thoughtful. I'm on pins and needles myself."

"Paul Shenstone's record," Edith went on, "is a distinguished one. Mentioned in dispatches 1915, decorated for bravery 1916, commissioned second lieutenant in 1917, and to top it off, the Military Cross in 1918."

"Mr. Shenstone, I had no idea we had such a decorated soldier in our midst." Lavinia again.

Morris managed not to wince.

"The citations are very nobly written," said Edith. "I read them, and then I went to Father's friend Colonel Paget to ask what it all means in words a girl can understand. Now don't interrupt: this part is important. Colonel Paget explained to me the horrors of trench warfare."

"Colonel Paget might have been in a trench for five minutes once," said Morris.

"Which he admitted," Edith replied. "But he explained as best he could about the shelling, the wet, the filth, the lice, the disease—what else?" She was counting off on her fingers, at which she stared with a frown of concentration.

"Oh, yes—the bad rations, the lack of sleep, the ill-conceived, ill-prepared attacks. And—most of all—the paralysis. For month after month, our fellows couldn't advance and weren't allowed to retreat. Military stagnation, moral stagnation, physical stagnation. Not every part of the Western Front was as muddy as Flanders, but it all felt, he said, like a quagmire. And it had our troops in its grip. So—the officers ordered trench raids to keep the men active and sharp. I can see Lavinia has the same question I had: what is a trench raid? It seems you cut your own wire at night, crawl across no man's land, cut the German wire, jump into their trenches and bring back prisoners for military intelligence to interrogate. No easy feat. Germans—strangely enough—don't always like being snatched out of their trenches. What do you do if you can't take prisoners? You cause what damage you can. You spread what terror you can. And you melt away into the night back to your own lines."

"Are you saying," asked Lavinia, "that what the citations add up to is that Mr. Shenstone was a trench raider?"

"A champion trench raider. Which means he is a champion at close-quarter homicide."

"Edie!" Lavinia exclaimed.

"Wait now," Edith cautioned. "I'm not being as presumptuous as you think. It was wartime. It was his duty. I'm not judging what Mr. Shenstone did in those dreadful years, which I lived through only in a cocooned and pampered childhood. If I had had his training and his strength, if I had been sent into those German trenches, I would possibly have cut as many throats as he did. What I say is this: of all the Canadian victims of the Peerless shells, none we know of died in the company of an older friend than did Horner Ingersoll. That friend was also one with a rare talent for killing men—in the dark of night—in the most intimate circumstances. A gunner, like Robert Taylor or Ivan MacAllister, likely took more lives throughout the war, but always at a distance. They never had to see those lives extinguished."

"You think I killed your father?" Edith was piquant to be sure, chattering of trench raids in her little convent-school dress. But I wasn't nearly as amused by her accusation as I tried to sound.

Edith didn't answer directly.

"Threats were uttered around the guns on the day of Ingersoll's death. Many were bluster, doubtless. But Mr. Shenstone, who said at the time that he wouldn't mind getting Mr. Peerless Armaments in a dark alley, showed by his conduct through the rest of the war that he would have known exactly what to do with Dad in that alley."

"Edith," Lavinia interjected, "I really must give you a scolding. What you say is not only discourteous but quite unreal. No man could be more clearly on the side of the forces of order than Mr. Shenstone. You have just finished telling us that he is a war hero. He's also a policeman."

"A policeman who was, as I learned this afternoon, not on duty the night Dad was shot. I don't know if Mr. Shenstone has an alibi. If so, I sincerely hope he'll break his Trappist vows to say so. Today I have learned that he had both the motive and the capacity to kill Digby Watt. Did he also have the opportunity? We wait to be instructed."

"Steady, Edith," Morris began. "It's one thing to point out that the sergeant has a personal interest in the case; it's quite another to suggest—"

But before he could get further with his protest, a soft insistent tapping at the open door to the hall momentarily caught everyone's attention. Nita stood there with a folded paper in her hand.

"Come in, Nita," said Morris. "What is it?"

Without looking left or right, the girl came to his chair and bent over to speak to him in an undertone.

"All right," said Morris, taking the paper from her hand and reading it.

Nita stood by his side with lowered eyes till he had done so. The women sent her curious looks, which remained unacknowledged.

"Thank you, Nita," said Morris. He took a pen from his jacket and scribbled something on the bottom of the paper before refolding it and handing it back to the housemaid. "Run along now."

Once she was out of the room, Morris rose definitively to his feet.

"Sergeant," he said, "there is no necessity for you to stay longer. If the police need more information from any member of this household, I would appreciate their phoning me at the office."

"I can't make any promises, Mr. Watt."

"No, I suppose not. Well, promises aren't what I'm looking for. I'll see you to your car."

Apparently it didn't occur to Digby's son and heir that one of the city's sixty thousand automobiles might not be at my disposal.

"But, Morris—"

"Later, Edith, please. Sergeant, I'm sorry..."

The furrows in Morris's forehead let it be understood that there were many things he was sorry about, including inviting me in so pressingly and throwing me out so abruptly. Plainly, he had not anticipated what Edith would say, let alone what was in the note. About all, Morris could be expected to have the most lively and anxious regrets, which in the circumstances were best left unspecified. The briefer the adieus, the less wretched Morris would be.

I tormented him only to the extent of approaching Lavinia's divan and accepting her extended hand. Edith did not offer hers, but whether from principle or distraction was not apparent. Even more surprising, in view of her suspicions, was the absence of any look of anger or dislike in the quizzical face she turned in my direction. Unpardonably, I winked at her as I left the room.

Chapter Fifteen

I rode away from the Watt residence with Ivan on my mind. On the one hand, Ivan had—of everyone connected with this case—what appeared to be the strongest corroboration of his story. On the other, he had had unique access to the crime scene. Everything came back to Ivan. Ivan's identification of a male voice on the telephone limited the range of suspects to men, or to women with male accomplices. Tinker's letter had been written by Ivan. Edith's suspicions of me had been started by Ivan.

Yes, Edith. I gunned the Harley-Davidson through a red light at Yonge and Bloor for absolutely no reason; it didn't make me feel any better.

Maybe I had been too soft on Ivan. Even if we hadn't served together, I had perhaps been moved by the freemasonry of battle, by our both being of those liable to a twitch in the gut when exposed to certain smells or noises, or even to the sound of certain European names. Ypres, Somme, Cambrai, Canal du Nord. It was sentimentality really. Time to put Ivan under some pressure.

The phone record corroboration of Ivan's story did not constitute, technically speaking, an alibi. By his own admission, Ivan had been alone with Digby Watt during the period in which Watt must have been killed. However, Ivan could not have been on both ends of the call that Bell Telephone said had been made at 1:44. If Ivan had been in his apartment at 1:44, someone had phoned him from

Sheppard Street. If Ivan had been at Adelaide and Sheppard at 1:44, someone else had been in his apartment.

I decided to test the latter hypothesis. As soon as I got back to the police station, I applied for a search warrant. Poking about the newsman's apartment would give me something to do while uniformed officers were getting hold of the cab driver Tony Bellotto and inviting Tinker and Ivan down to City Hall for questioning.

Dusk was drawing in as I parked in front of a row of shops on the west side of Broadview just north of Danforth. Search warrants had to be executed during the day, but day extended for legal purposes till nine p.m. There was a milliner's, a real estate office, a grocery and a barber shop, as well as Bull Moose Sporting Goods. The suite above the latter had a separate entrance, a freshly painted black wooden door. Locked. When I pressed the button, I could hear a bell ring somewhere on the other side. I knocked anyway, for good measure. The door stayed shut. When I stepped back and looked up, I could see no light in the bay window jutting over the sidewalk. I next rapped on the glass of the shop door. Although it was locked too, a light in the rear of the premises showed someone back there sitting over a ledger. Gold lettering on the glass led me to believe this was Hermann Vogel, prop.—a hunch he confirmed when he came to see what the commotion was, and I showed him my badge.

"I see you sell firearms," I said. "Do you have any vest-pocket automatics?"

Vogel, a short man whose hair was receding and whose stomach was straining at the buttons of his tartan vest, sniffed that guns like these had no sporting use.

MacAllister had been renting from him for four years, ever since Vogel had been able to afford a house and stop living over the shop. The only occasions on which landlord and tenant spoke were when Ivan was late with the rent. They spoke often. Vogel recounted this fact with irritation, but hastened to add that he always got paid by the fifth of the month. He felt MacAllister to be careless in a lordly way rather than seriously insolvent. A good risk, therefore, provided one were willing to put in the work of nagging him.

My request to be admitted to Ivan's apartment made Vogel wary.

"What sort of trouble is he in?"

"No sort that I know of," I said. "But he's a witness in the Watt murder. We're having a word with him at the station, and I need to pick up some of his papers."

"So he knows you're here?"

"Everything's perfectly in order, Mr. Vogel."

I waved the warrant in front of Vogel's face, without offering to let him read it. The document identified indecent photographs as the object of police interest, and there was no need yet to embarrass Ivan to that degree.

Apparently satisfied, Vogel led me upstairs. The apartment was compact, with a living-dining room on the street side. A kitchen, bath and bedroom overlooked the back alley.

"Does he ever have overnight visitors, Mr. Vogel?"

"Maybe. I'm not here that late, and I don't worry if a red-blooded male brings a girl back to his place from time to time. As long as there aren't two people living here full time, you get me? With two living here, I'd be entitled to more rent."

"Naturally," I said. "Would you know if Mr. MacAllister had a woman here the night before last?"

"That would have been Monday. No, I couldn't say.

That's the night I teach fly tying at the Temagami Club, so I went home for dinner sharp at closing time."

"I'll let you get back to your accounts tonight then. Just tell me if you want to leave before I do, in case I have more questions."

Vogel puffed off down the stairs, and I began my search. Of course, I would have loved to find three .25 ACP cartridge cases. But I was also looking for any evidence of a second person's presence in the apartment. Ivan explained his being found at the deceased's side by the phone call made to this apartment on the night of the murder. If he had made that call himself, there would have had to be someone to pick up the receiver here

As at Glen Road, a hefty radio occupied pride of place in the living area—but Ivan's was a more recent model, a Rogers Batteryless plugged into a light socket. At the same end of the room sat an equally up-to-date gramophone. A bank of shelves held a few dozen jazz recordings and piles of magazines separated according to title and stacked in order of date, with the oldest at the bottom and the newest on top.

At the other end of the room, the dining table bore the journalist's two most important tools, a telephone and a typewriter. The remaining surface areas were covered by typing supplies, reference books and typescript piled according to project. One of these projects appeared to be a war story of some sort, whether a novel or a memoir I couldn't tell. The title was *We Shall Not Sleep.*

I read a paragraph at random—

They blame the blunders, the Sommes, the Passchendaeles, on poor communication. It was a war of great chemical and mechanical sophistication (read maxim guns and phosgene gas) in which messages were carried by pigeons. Pigeons, for Christ's sake. Oh, yes, they'll blaspheme a little to express their frustration that there were as yet no compact two-way radios. Think of the lives that could have been saved! And yet, the generals' tears are tears of laughter at their dupes. Next time you hear them profanely compassionate, remind them they had unused mobile observation posts in the sky. I never yet heard of a general's risking his neck by going up in an airplane to reconnoitre troop positions. Think of the lives they could have saved if they had. For Jesus Christ's bleeding sake.

Bitter, I thought. Shows a spirit capable of killing Digby Watt. Ivan wrote exactly what I felt. Of course, for Ivan, the bitterness could all be a fashionable pose.

The middle of the room was occupied by a comfortable green sofa, long enough that a woman might feel safe at one end of it, short enough for the man at the other end to reach her side by the time she had taken the first sip of her cocktail. I looked under the cushions and on the floor. Nothing hidden or mislaid.

I spent another half hour in the living room before tackling the kitchen.

The only thing of interest about the kitchen was that it doubled as a darkroom. The window was fitted with a totally light-proof blind, the door equally sealed against light, and a red bulb installed in the ceiling beside the regular kitchen fixture. Developing and printing chemicals were stored under the sink, papers in one of the cupboards. The refrigerator contained film as well as the few foods stocked by a bachelor who dislikes cooking.

So Ivan was not only a photographer, but one in a position to take pictures no one else need see or approve. Wherever he kept these interesting documents, they weren't in the kitchen. Neither did I see any cameras, which perhaps he borrowed from the *Examiner* to keep expenses down.

The bathroom yielded two razors, with traces of different shades of stubble. Mud-brown—from Ivan's chin. And dark chocolate—from his lady's armpits, perhaps. The first sign of an overnight guest.

I attacked the bedroom, prepared to find a flimsy nightdress tucked into the corner of a dresser drawer or a little frock hanging in the closet between suits. Nothing doing. The only jarring note in the closet was a pair of work pants with slush-stained cuffs. I wondered why they stood out.

It was because the season had changed some weeks ago. These pants must have remained unwashed for over a month. Now Ivan was no spit and polish homemaker. I could see he didn't bother much with a duster or a carpet sweeper or even an iron. He was organized, however—far better than I am. The bed was made, dishes washed, litter tidied away. The laundry hamper was no more than a quarter full. And these khaki pants weren't in it. Nothing else in the closet was visibly soiled.

Perhaps it meant nothing. These were pants for messy jobs, such as even a toff might have tucked away somewhere. And then again, they bore no signs of messy jobs. No paint stains, for example.

I held them up beside another pair of slacks from the closet. The waists were of quite different measurements. Indeed, every pair of trousers in the apartment was marked thirty-two inches, except for the soiled pair. Which were forty-fours. When could Ivan MacAllister's waist ever have been that size?

I turned my attention to a corner of the bedroom occupied by a grey metal filing cabinet. Top drawer: research notes and news clippings. Middle drawer: financial statements. Bottom drawer: a series of folders labelled Premium, Regular Price, Discount, Deep Discount, Two-for-one and Remainders, each folder stuffed with photographic prints and negatives catering to every sexual taste I'd heard of and some I hadn't. Here was how the crime writer financed his little luxuries—his Bulova watch, his Batteryless radio. That he wasn't yet living in a house the size of Watt's showed either decorous restraint or that he was just getting started.

Chapter Sixteen

Tinker had been waiting an hour and a half in the interrogation room by the time I got down to police headquarters. He was also missing a second night's work in a row and feared for his livelihood. He was far too angry to talk to, so I let him wait some more and went first to question Ivan. Ivan, I gathered, had only been waiting half as long.

Have I mentioned how cramped our premises at City Hall were? There was a closed-off room—one—in which we could question suspects without actually throwing them in a cell, and I got some dirty looks and nasty comments from my colleagues for leaving my man Taylor in exclusive possession of this one princely chamber for so long. What concerned me more about the situation was that there had been no place to put Ivan, who had to be kept out of contact with Tinker. The journalist had been left sitting by my desk in the middle of the detectives' room.

"Thanks for coming in, Ivan."

"Being invited to eavesdrop on HQ is a rare treat. I no longer have to wonder what to write for the Saturday edition."

I set a closed paper bag containing the size forty-four trousers and a selection of Ivan's photos on top of my desk. I was relieved to see that the only document I'd left out there was yesterday's newspaper.

"What I was wondering," I said, "was whether there's

anything you'd like to change in that account you wrote of the night before last."

"Why should there be?" Ivan's long limbs were folded comfortably over one another, and he was enjoying a cigarette. An ashtray he had scrounged from somewhere was already full of the butts of its predecessors.

I did not sit down right away, but stood beside him, my right shoe on the rung of his chair. I kept my voice low.

"Have you been talking to Edith Watt?"

"Sounds as if you know I have," Ivan replied. "She called me."

"And you've been suggesting to her that I might be her father's murderer."

"No. I pointed out that you knew Horny better than any of us."

"Was mine the voice you heard on the phone that night? The voice that told you to go to 96 Adelaide Street West?"

"I don't know. Was it?"

"You don't know?"

"Remember I'd only met you once, Paul, very briefly, and that was eleven years ago. At the time, I was thinking more about Horny than about what you sounded like. It's a pretty typical mid-range voice anyhow—southern Ontario, no British or foreign accent. Literate with a shot of 'plain folks' to avoid being thought too stuck up."

"Fancy footwork, Ivan, and almost convincing. Except that we met yesterday morning, less than ten hours after you got the phone call. If I had made that call, you would have found my voice familiar right away."

"I was woken from a sound sleep. I was groggy. I can't swear it was you. I can't swear it wasn't."

"Can you swear it was a man's?"

"Are there women suspected? Oh, I see. You want to pay

Edith Watt back for accusing you. But what will you do for a motive? Did she have debts?"

"Could it have been a woman's voice, Ivan?"

"I doubt it. And, unless she's off her head, Edith would never have left her father waving in the breeze like that."

"Miss Watt is not under discussion here." The chair rung splintered under my weight. I came around behind Ivan, forcing him to twist his neck to see me. "Even if you really got this phone call, Ivan, even if you didn't shoot Digby Watt, you could have had your petty measure of revenge. You're still angry enough about the war to have done that, aren't you?"

Ivan wasn't letting himself get rattled this time as he had yesterday morning. I leaned over him.

"Aren't you, for Jesus Christ's bleeding sake?"

Ivan's mud-coloured moustache twitched.

"Yes, I went through your apartment and saw that valentine you're writing to the generals. And you know what else I found, don't you? I found that, on film at least, male anatomy is something you're quite used to handling."

"You're a nasty piece of work, Paul."

"The minute I saw that green sofa in your living room, I thought seduction. I just didn't picture a man at each end and you in close to follow their progress through a view finder."

"I had no score to settle with Digby Watt," Ivan sputtered, "not by the end of the war. But I sure as hell have a score to settle with you."

Several heads turned our way, including that of the stenographer Lindstrom.

"Need a hand, sergeant?" he asked, without any apparent intention that the hand should be his.

"Intimidation by threat can result in jail time with hard

labour, Ivan. I'll give you some time to reconsider. Yes, Lindstrom, I do. Make sure this man doesn't leave his chair."

"But, sergeant, I'm not..."

Guffaws from one or two of my detective colleagues.

"Don't razz him now," I told them. "He'll do fine."

I took the paper bag from my desk to Tinker's interrogation room. It was a small room and hot; cracks and pops from the radiator meant it was getting hotter. The light bulbs were low wattage and further dimmed by dust. The window looked across the dark courtyard at other windows, all but a couple of which were dark at this hour. The table wobbled. All three chairs were broken, though one seemed capable of supporting Tinker's weight if he kept very still. There was no other furniture.

"Tinker, I'm sorry about all this. If you help me out, I'll talk to them at the Alhambra and make sure you keep your job. Just try these on for me, will you? I'll wait outside."

I saw the big man's jaw drop and nothing more before I was out in the hall again. When I returned, Tinker had done as he was told. He had been wearing his work clothes, a large but still tight tuxedo. The khaki pants with the stained cuffs were a much more comfortable-looking fit.

"I know what you mean, Tinker, about its being a bad time for alibis—the hours between 1:30 a.m. and 2:30. Either you live with a family member who would lie to protect you, or you live alone with no one to say whether you slipped out in the wee hours to do a little murder. Or, most maddening of all, you have a witness right in the bed with you, but you're not anxious to have it known. It would be embarrassing for one or both of you, maybe expose you to the risk of prosecution on a morality charge. And would the testimony of a sodomite do you any good in court anyway?"

"What the Sam Hill are you talking about, Paul?"

"Ivan's already let the cat out of the bag. No need for you to protect him. I told him I found those pants of yours in his apartment—the ones you left behind when you put on the new grey flannels he gave you. And he admitted you were there the night before last when the phone rang."

"He what?"

"Don't think I mind. But the law takes a narrower view of these things. We don't want to put you through another trial, risk landing you in Kingston. So your best course is to work with me as much as you can."

"This morning we were drinking coffee together, and tonight you're threatening me with the Pen. You bastard!"

"That sweet stuff's wasted on me. Just tell me everything about the phone call you took at 1:44 on the morning of the twentieth."

"Ivan took it."

"No, you don't have to tell that story any more. Ivan says it's all right if you tell me the truth." I picked Tinker's black work trousers off the table and began folding them neatly.

"Hey, what are you doing with those, Paul? Put them down. I need them for work."

"And you'll get them back when you've come clean. Think about it." I went to the door, the trousers still in my hands. "Remember, if you took the call, you couldn't have done the murder. You do have an alibi."

This was not quite the truth. But Tinker held up his great beefy, pianistic hands in a gesture of surrender.

"Okay, it was me. I answered the phone."

"Take your time."

"They said, 'Ivan, is that a foreign name?' I said no. They said to go to 96 Adelaide Street West. That was it."

"Why did you take the call?"

"I was sleeping on the sofa. I was nearer the phone."

"On the sofa? I'll bet. Where was Ivan?"

"In the bedroom."

"It wasn't his voice on the phone?"

"How could it be? He was in his frigging room, and he came out to see what was happening before I'd even hung up."

"Did you recognize the voice?"

"No."

"Would you recognize it if you heard it again?"

"How do you mean?"

"If, for example, I were to say to you, 'Go to 96 Adelaide Street West,' would you be able to say whether I was the caller?"

"No. I mean—no, it wasn't you. Was it?"

"Was the voice a man's or a woman's?"

"A man's. No, I'm not sure. It could have been a woman's."

"Think it over," I said.

I packed Tinker's work trousers into my paper bag and returned to my desk. The stenographer was standing watch at some distance.

"Sergeant," he said, "the taxi driver is out in the corridor."

"Ask him please to go back to his cab, park it in front of the main steps, and sit in it. Explain we're a little short of space here, and say I'll be out as soon as I can."

Ivan was still seated where I'd left him, though he looked jumpy. His empty Players cigarette pack sat on the desk beside him. He was writing in a notebook, which he made vanish into his pocket when I approached.

"Things are looking bad for you, Ivan. Tinker's in another room, and he's confessed that he's the one who took that call in your apartment the night before last."

"What?"

"Don't think he betrayed you. He had no choice. But you see the problem, don't you? If you didn't answer the call—the phone call that shows up so conveniently on the phone company's books—you could have made it."

"No."

"Sure you could. In time I'll get the whole story out of Tinker, but it'll sound better coming from you."

"I was at home at 1:45. If that cab driver you've got waiting outside is the one that picked me up from in front of Bull Moose, ask him."

"Did the cab driver get a good look at you? Will he be able to swear it was you and not Tinker?"

Ivan was not his usual glib self and did not seem to have a ready answer.

"Am I under arrest?" he said.

"Not at present. You can leave—but you might want to stay and talk about how we can keep news of your photographic sideline from reaching the *Examiner*. I'm not saying they'd publish a story on it, but your newspaper career might get edited down to zero."

Ivan bit his right thumbnail. Then he looked at it and was about to bite it again, but changed his mind. Instead, he stood up and stuck his hands in his pockets. I wasn't as comfortable with him standing, but thought I'd see what came of it.

"Do you have any cigarettes?" he asked. "Never mind—forget it. I'll tell you what happened. You can believe it or not. Tinker came over after he finished work at the cinema. It got late, so he stayed the night."

I let that lie.

"Nothing extraordinary there. We were battery mates."

"If battery mates give each other Savile Row trousers," I couldn't help saying, "I guess I've plenty to learn about gunners' lore."

"The flannel slacks were a fee for some modelling work he'd done, okay? We were both asleep by one, I in my bed, Tinker on the sofa. The phone is in the living room, so when it rang, he picked up the receiver."

"If that's what happened, why didn't you say so before?"

"It made a simpler story if I was alone. Look, whatever Tinker is, or whatever he's told you, I'm not a homosexual. It just would have given the wrong idea to say I had him stay the night."

"Wouldn't it have ruined your simple story if it had been your paper calling and Tinker answered the phone?"

"I don't say he was thinking clearly. The phone woke him up. He wanted to make it stop ringing. I hadn't told him not to answer it, so he answered it."

I thought that sounded like Tinker all right. I tried not to smile.

"Were you even in your apartment when Tinker picked up the phone?"

"Yes."

"Or," I pursued, "did you leave him there while you went downtown? Did you in fact go to a public telephone at Adelaide and Sheppard and *make* that call to your apartment, the call that Tinker answered at about a quarter to two? Remember: any story you tell has to jibe with Tinker's."

"Paul—I was in my bed, alone, when the phone rang. Tinker was on the sofa. By the time I got out to the living room, Tinker had picked up the receiver."

I took the sepia-toned photos from the paper bag. They constituted a sampling from the bottom drawer of Ivan's filing cabinet. The first eight by ten print was of two men, both unknown to me, engaged in mutual masturbation.

"That's quite a photographic collection you've amassed," I observed.

"Fine art stuff, some of it quite experimental."

"What the courts would call obscenity. Producing or distributing it could get you locked up for as long as two years—and considering how deviant your art is, you shouldn't count on much less."

"I wouldn't expect you to understand."

"Sit!"

He did. So did I.

"I'll never understand anything, Ivan, if you keep lying to me. You lied about taking that phone call. You also lied about not taking a camera to 96 Adelaide Street West." I held up a second eight by ten, this one of Digby Watt on his back with dark stains on his waistcoat and his genitals hanging out. "That was another way of simplifying the story, wasn't it? But the simplest story of all would be for you to just tell me now that you're the one that killed him. You, Ivan. Then you posed him for a portrait that would strip his death of any shred of dignity."

"I didn't, though. I mean, sure, I took the photo. That was an opportunity not to be missed. But the man was too insignificant for me to risk my neck on his account."

"Not too insignificant to make you good and sore. I've read the 'Mr. Peerless' letter you wrote for Tinker to put his name to and send to Digby Watt."

"Tinker was out of work at the time. We were just trying to get Watt to give him a leg up."

I wiped the photo with my hand.

"That was no begging letter," I said. "That was an indictment. Come on, Ivan, tell me how it happened. You'll never find a more sympathetic ear to pour your confession into. You and I both know Peerless deserved to die."

"If that's what you think, Paul, you confess."

I wiped the photo again. It was like having some shred of food stuck between my teeth, distracting me from my line of questions. My hand kept brushing across the matte paper. What was I trying to get rid of? Bits of dust or lint? But no, there was no dust, no lint; those dots—oblongs, really—were part of the scene. And were exactly what I should be looking at.

"Let's have them, Ivan."

"What?"

"Sure, there are places in your apartment you might have hidden them, but I'm betting you carry them around with you. Hand them over."

"What are you talking about?"

"The cartridge cases, Leonardo. I can see two of them in your 'fine art' photo, and I'm sure you looked around and managed to pick up the third."

"I don't have them."

"Of course you have them. I can't believe how much trouble you've got yourself into. You take a picture, and they're with the body: they must have bounced back off the building. The constable arrives, and they're nowhere to be seen. You were the only person there. Where could they have gone if not into your pocket?"

"The murderer—the murderer could have come back for them while I was phoning the police."

"Desperate words from a desperate man. Why would he do that, Ivan?"

"Because—because, if they have the shells, your ballistics men can trace the gun. The murderer might have forgot that, then realized after he left the scene that he couldn't afford to leave evidence lying around."

"The murderer was you, Ivan MacAllister. You were just cleaning up after yourself."

"No. Remember I was home with Tinker when the murderer called."

"An alibi provided by your lover. Worthless!"

Glistening beads of sweat stood on Ivan's forehead.

"I'd like a glass of water," he said.

"I'll bet," I replied. "Are you going to tell me you just took those cases as souvenirs?"

"No."

"Then you took them to protect the murderer."

"I didn't take them."

"I'm satisfied that you did. Satisfied enough that I'm going to arrest you right now. That will give me the right to go through your pockets, where I'll find those cases. And I'll get to read your notebook as well."

Ivan's hand came out of his pocket and emptied three brass shells onto the table.

"Do you have a quarter?" I asked.

"What? Why?"

"I'll ask the constable that runs these up to the lab to buy you smokes on the way back."

Chapter Seventeen

Sitting in his cab on Queen Street West, Tony Bellotto was obliged to turn away potential fares and see the business he was missing. It wasn't till after ten p.m. that I at last had a chance to go out and speak to him. I found his black Ford close to the foot of the City Hall steps and climbed into the front seat beside him. He was a short man with black, curly hair. A bit of a dandy by the look of his leather jacket and purple shirt. He was young, early to mid twenties, and understandably impatient.

"How long have you been working nights, Mr. Bellotto?" I asked.

"Since before Christmas, beginning of December."

"You must see pretty well in the dark." I scribbled a random sequence of numbers on a scrap of paper and dropped it in the back seat. I figured the street lighting was about the same here as on Adelaide, or Broadview for that matter. "How much of that can you read?"

He read all the numbers backwards in the rear view mirror and called them out forwards.

"Good enough, Mr. Bellotto. Now five men will be sent out here to us one at a time. Each one will get into the back of your cab, give you an address, and get out again. You're not to say anything or give any sign while any of the men are in the car. Understood?"

"Sure."

"All right. When you've seen all five, I want you to tell

me which one, if any, is the passenger you picked up at 2:01 on the morning of April 20 outside Bull Moose Sporting Goods. Questions?"

"Can we get started?"

My parade included both Tinker and Ivan, but kept apart to avoid mutual recriminations. For the other three, I had collected a lanky car thief from the lock-up and from the detectives' room the two men with the most substantial build. Ivan was unequivocally identified as the passenger Bellotto had driven to 96 Adelaide Street West. Tinker was then allowed to leave with both pairs of trousers.

Back at my desk, on the phone to the manager of the Alhambra, I conveyed that Robert Taylor had been offering the police invaluable assistance with an investigation, without being either charged with or suspected of any crime, and it would be taken most kindly if his absence this evening from his post at the piano could be overlooked. The manager, clearly no poker player, asked if this had anything to do with "that business of the fire regulations"—at which point I knew Tinker would stay clear of soup kitchens a while longer.

Ivan was in a less fortunate position. I now had enough evidence to charge him under either section 207 or section 267 or both of the Criminal Code of Canada. By rights, I should already have handed the photographs I'd found in his apartment over to the judge issuing the search warrant, but the more serious offence by far was concealing evidence. That had made Ivan an accessory after the fact to murder.

Although I still preferred to postpone arresting him, the threat was enough to induce him to turn out his pockets. The only weapon found on him was the clasp knife he had been playing with after Horny's death. I took possession of it and let him keep everything else. I then allowed him to order in some coffee to go with his cigarettes and gave him a chance to wash up before resuming our talk in the now vacant interrogation room.

"Why did you take those shells?" I began.

Ivan sat hunched over the unsteady table, his forearms resting on it. He was watching my face closely. He appeared aware of the seriousness of his position. If this were a pose, it was the right pose.

"I'm a crime reporter," he said. "I know cartridge cases are the best way to trace a gun. The bullets themselves bear unique rifling marks, but the bullets are often deformed by the impact."

"Who shot Digby Watt?"

"I don't know. Honestly, Paul."

"Yet you admit to helping the murderer."

"Whoever killed Watt may not have realized the value of what he was leaving behind. I just thought I'd give the hand of vengeance a little camouflage."

"Meanwhile throwing away your freedom and your career. Some thought."

"I was careless. How did you know I took pictures?"

"The sepia toner on your fingers. I figured it was nicotine at first, but the pattern was wrong. Pornographers should use tongs."

"I was careless and dumb—but if it hadn't been for the incredible coincidence of your being the investigating officer, Paul, I'd never have come under suspicion. No other detective would have known I had any feeling about Watt one way or the other."

"How much of a feeling was it, Ivan? Did you take the gun as well?"

"No. There was no gun there."

I laid the Spanish pocket pistol on the table in front of

him. I saw Ivan's eyes take it in, then direct a brief look of contempt at me. Contempt, not guilt.

"If you found that in my apartment, it wasn't me that put it there."

"Tinker?"

"Tinker hasn't come to my place since the murder. Besides, I can't imagine a little toy like that in Tinker's mitt. Can you?"

"Pretty deadly toy. Have you ever seen it before?" I handed Ivan the gun. He took it in his handkerchief.

"How would I know? I've seen guns like it."

"How recently have you seen one like it?"

"In the past week."

"When in the past week?"

"Yesterday."

I whistled my surprise. Was it possible I had a witness?

"Yesterday in the early hours?" I asked. "In front of 96 Adelaide Street West?"

"No, later, just after eleven p.m.—and not there."

"Where?"

"I don't—"

"Yes, you do."

"In a blind pig—if you won't hold that against me. In a cocotte's handbag."

I felt as if I had swallowed a mouthful of rancid butter.

"Which blind pig?"

Only a short hesitation. "The Lacombes' joint, in the old Reliable Cartage stables."

I thought hard about that. I didn't like his knowing May. What I couldn't make his knowing her add up to was any involvement by May in Watt's murder. Ivan wasn't selling out a confederate, merely trying to deflect suspicion onto an easy target.

Ivan's lips weren't smiling, but his smirky little eyes showed he knew he had got to me. His choice of a French word was a sly reminder that he and I had both served in Europe and were men of the world. He could see I resented the intimacy, and—despite the jail time he faced—that made him cocky.

"Smells like this has been fired, Paul. Is it the murder weapon?"

Before I could bite his head off, there was a knock at the interview room door, and an apple-cheeked boy walked in.

"Hope I'm not interrupting, sergeant. Inspector Sanderson would like a word."

I swept the stripling out the door and shut it behind us.

"The surest way to find out whether you're interrupting," I growled, "is to wait outside a closed door for permission to enter. Now who are you?"

His already rosy face turned redder under his straight blonde hair.

"Acting Detective Ned Cruickshank, sir. From Station Number One. I've been working with you on the Digby Watt murder. Guess we've never been in the office at the same time, but you may have read my reports. Incidentally, the ex-chauffeur Webster has an alibi, ironclad. Sorry to burst in on you—"

"Okay, Ned. I needed a rest from that bird. You carrying a flask?"

Cruickshank was too shocked to answer, but I could imagine if there were a flask in any pocket of his glaringly cheap new suit, it would be full of milk. When I'd been permitted to make the switch from uniforms to plain clothes, I received a dress allowance of ten cents a day. I doubted if the figure was much more generous now.

"No whisky? It's a shame to put men in the field without

equipment. Now look, Ned: the crime reporter Ivan MacAllister is behind this door. I've already had a look around his apartment, but I want you to take him to the *Examiner* office and search anywhere he might be able to keep anything at all. Don't let him see you blush at what you find. Above all, make sure he destroys nothing. His desk is to be emptied, and everything that is not his employer's property brought to me."

"Should I get a search warrant first, in case he makes problems?"

"He removed the cartridge cases from the murder scene and can be charged at any time as an accessory. Maximum penalty: life. Keep that possibility before him, and you should find him pliant. You'll be arresting him anyway as soon as you get him back here, but he doesn't have to know that. Let him live in hope."

"All right, sergeant. Is he the murderer?"

"Everything but, worse luck. Grill him a bit more while you're out. What, apart from the shells, did he touch while he was alone with Watt?"

"Ah—yes, sergeant," Cruickshank stammered. "By the way, the inspector—"

"I'm just going. For once, I'll have something to tell him."

Inspector Sanderson wasn't prepared to listen to what I had to say until he had got off his chest his unhappiness at having to hear from Morris Watt about my old grudge against Peerless Armaments.

"So are you reassigning me?" I said as soon as I could shoehorn a word in.

"I've reassigned Knight instead," Sanderson huffed from the middle of clouds of tarry pipe smoke. "You and Cruickshank are going to complete this assignment to my satisfaction. Can we make that Curtis chap swing?"

"We haven't enough on him yet. But we've got the cartridge cases."

"That's nothing unless they lead us to the gun. Where did you get them?"

"The newspaperman took them."

"Your old acquaintance, as I now discover—columnist for the *Examiner*." Sanderson smacked his lips over the name of the paper he was so tired of hearing praised in his own home. His eyebrows bristled. "The bright light that started this 'Who's next?' scare. Let's string *him* up. He had what he supposed was a motive—and it's the motive that best explains sabotaging the Gray-Dort. I've always thought that was a needless frill. If all the murderer wanted was to kill Watt, there'd have been time enough while Morris Watt was fetching the car, even if the car was sound. The pin must have been pulled out just to be cute. Bum shell, bum car—see?"

"Won't wash," I said. "The taxi driver gives him what amounts to an alibi. Ivan arrived on the scene no more than five minutes ahead of Morris Watt. In five minutes, he'd have had to hustle to photograph the corpse—yes, sir, he did—then tuck the camera and flash equipment back in his rucksack and pick up the shells. But he couldn't count on having even five minutes. How was he to know that Morris would wander off to call a taxi *before* he returned to tell his father about the trouble with the Gray-Dort? Morris might have arrived back in front of 96 Adelaide Street West a good four or five minutes sooner—before MacAllister even. The conclusion is inescapable: the sabotage of the car shows that Digby Watt's murder was planned, and if Ivan had planned it, he would have given himself more time."

“You haven’t told MacAllister he’s no longer a suspect, have you?”

“No, sir.”

“Then convince the taxi driver he must be wrong. It was dark. His eyesight is bad.”

“Nope. I gave him an eye test.”

“His eyes must be bad. Or he’s bad with faces. Explain what a public service he’d be performing. The forces of law and order would look good. The public would feel safer.”

I laughed.

“Honestly, Paul.”

“Help innocent folk sleep better by sending an innocent man to the gallows?”

“Doubtless he’s [illegible]”

“Guilty of something else. Yes, inspector, in this case that’s true. MacAllister’s guilty of concealing evidence, and that’s serious enough to make me think we shouldn’t let him out of here tonight. But it’s a non-capital offence. Ivan MacAllister took the shells; he did not kill Digby Watt. Look on the bright side, sir. You’ve got the conspiracy you’ve been looking for, after all—although possibly an unplanned one.”

“I’d say you have a soft spot for an army pal. Toughen up, sergeant.”

“Gunners had their uses, sir, but they weren’t infantry. For MacAllister in particular, I’ve a feeling about as warm as for the dirt on my shoe. I wish he *had* done this murder. He didn’t do it, though, and I won’t frame him for it.”

Sanderson set down his pipe and pinched his lower lip.

“Paul,” he resumed in an avuncular tone, “I don’t like it when I have to hear from a murdered man’s son what I should be hearing from my own men. Why didn’t you tell me about this Ingersoll business?”

"I don't like to talk about the war."

"What's liking got to do with it? And where were you anyway between one thirty and two thirty on the morning of the twentieth?"

"You're fingering me for Watt's murder?" I asked, once I'd massaged my dropped jaw back into working order.

"Certainly not, Paul—but if your conscience is troubling you, confession is good for the soul."

I let that opportunity pass.

"What I'm getting at," the inspector continued, "is that frequenting a bar or house of ill-fame except in the line of duty is a firing offence, and one I'm less likely to overlook in unproductive officers."

"Thanks for the reminder," I said, at this point almost indifferent to whether I stayed a cop. "May I remind the inspector in turn that an average year sees three murders in this town? Two of the three are murder-suicides and the third so well witnessed that no sleuthing is required. In view of the circumstances of *yesterday's* murder, I respectfully submit that your detective force has not been dragging its heels. Now, if you'll excuse me, I think I'll go home and get some sleep. Just so you know where to send the notice of dismissal."

I asked around the office what they thought Sanderson's hurry was. Knight said the detective inspector's brother-in-law was planning to use the Saturday edition of the *Examiner* to offer an expense-paid private bodyguard to any company president on Bay Street, with the implication that the police were incapable of keeping the business community safe. For the honour of the department, Sanderson meant to frustrate this stunt with an arrest before the weekend. I stopped asking after that.

I was pretty fed up. I didn't go home, though. I found I

could get the case out of my mind all right, but not the phrase "in a cocotte's handbag". I went through the rest of the photographs I'd removed from Ivan's apartment. Those in the Premium folder, like that of Digby Watt, seemed to have been taken for personal rather than for commercial reasons. Ivan used himself more often as a model, as if he were enacting his own fantasies, with partners both male and female. But the picture I was looking for and dreading wasn't there. I didn't get it until, about an hour later, Cruickshank brought me the contents of Ivan's desk.

It was in its own brown envelope, marked "not currently for sale". It was of May on her knees looking up at the photographer with the photographer's long penis well down her throat, her lipstick-enhanced lips wrapped snugly around the shaft. She wore a black silk mask, but I recognized the mole halfway down the right side of her nose. And the sweet, cheeky look in her eyes.

Ivan had been with her last night. Just after eleven p.m., he'd said. That's when he'd seen the gun in her handbag. The picture might have been taken on another day entirely, or minutes before I arrived at Dolores and Ernie's. I closed my eyes, but found I liked what I saw then even less. If I'd put anything in my stomach since lunch, it would have come up.

Cruickshank was sitting across from me, fussing with some magnesium flash powder found in another of Ivan's desk drawers, making too obvious an effort not to look at the photo. When my phone rang, he beat me to it.

"Yes... Yes, sir. Could you hold on a moment, please?" With his hand over the mouthpiece, he said, "It's Professor Linacre, sergeant, calling about those cartridge cases. He thinks an Italian gun—"

I snatched the phone out of the acting detective's hand.

"Shenstone here, professor. Can I have that once more?"

"Yes. As I say, marks left by the extractor and traces from the ejector are most consistent with rounds fired from a Beretta semi-automatic pocket pistol, the Model 1919. They couldn't possibly have come from the Spanish Prince you fired into my box this afternoon."

Entr'acte

Police work has taught me that even when people end up telling you everything you need, they rarely tell it in the order you'd prefer to hear it. The most painful part of the story has to be worked up to or dragged out of them.

I don't like to talk about the war. It doesn't help that, when I do, I catch myself using sporty little fig-leaf phrases, like "a hot time in the Salient".

"I was out of the line," I said in relating Horny's death, "but I'd just been through a hot time in the Salient, and my nerves were still pretty taut."

Let me translate. If a peninsula is a body of land almost completely surrounded by water, the Salient was from 1914 to 1918 a Belgian bog almost completely surrounded by German artillery. In the middle stood Ypres, the only city of Belgium the invader couldn't get his hands on. He could get his shells on it all right, though, each big one weighing a ton before exploding. He could kill or drive out the inhabitants and turn buildings like the Cloth Hall that had stood for centuries to rubble. But as the practical value of Ypres fell, its symbolic value loomed larger and larger, and we had to fight for it all the harder.

It wasn't fighting either, not for the 48th Highlanders of Canada on April 24, 1915. What was it? It was meekly delivering one's quivering flesh to the worst suffering that machines and chemicals could be made to inflict.

The spring dawn broke clear and fair. The famous Flanders mud, so inescapable in winter, played no part on this particular day: all the vileness was man-made. At four a.m., we saw a number of grotesque heads in deep-sea diver's gear appear over the German parapet. Each man had in his hand a hose from which yellow greenish smoke began to flow and merge into a wall of cloud, a smoke rampart blown gently towards us on the morning breeze. We started firing, of course, but you feel pretty helpless shooting at a cloud. We had three minutes to wonder if we were going to be able to stick it out, standing to on our firing steps, waiting to be poisoned. Two days before, the first German gas attack of the war—the first gas attack in history—had routed two French divisions and sent them scurrying to the rear.

Three minutes, and the cloud was upon us, a wave of vapour fifteen to twenty feet high. Inside the cloud everything was green, as if we had put on tinted glasses. We'd been told to hold water- or urine-soaked pads of cloth over nose and mouth. Those pads did nothing to keep the gas from attacking our eyes, burning and blurring whatever we might still have seen through the green filter. And the pads didn't keep the gas out of our lungs either, though it must have slowed it down, for the men who didn't take this precaution were the first to fall to the bottom of the trench. Heavier than air, the chlorine followed them down to the duck-boards and finished its work on them where they lay writhing. They coughed up a glue-like substance which I guess had been their lungs, and soon enough they lay still, with bubbles of blood clustered at their nostrils and thick strings of saliva trailing from their lips.

My piss-soaked hanky was saturated with gas soon enough. My own lungs were burning, and my head ached.

I could do nothing where I stood and was becoming disoriented. Somehow I managed to stagger leftwards down the trench with some other members of number three company and emerge from the edge of the cloud. My nose was running, and my throat felt scraped raw. Engine noises overhead directed my attention up, and I was able to make out a big airplane with black crosses on its wings. From his godlike perch, the observer was doubtless taking note that some of us ants were still crawling about down here, and preparing to instruct his artillery accordingly. Lost in contemplating this new threat, I was blocking traffic in the narrow trench. Unknown hands pulled me along and poured some rum down my throat. So help me, it was the first drink of my life. The number of total abstainers in our regiment declined as the war dragged on—but when we landed on the Continent, I was far from the only 48th Highlander who had never touched a drop. Naturally, I choked. They poured some more spirits into me, and I revived enough to shoulder my gun.

The Germans were following up their poison cloud as closely as they dared, Mausers blazing. I fired at the attackers until my Ross rifle overheated and jammed, as the Ross rifle always did, and then I felt my eyes misting over again, but whether from gas or frustration, I couldn't have said. I was coughing all the while, and my spit was thick and salty in my mouth. My hands were cold. My chest felt tight, and I had to plan for the effort of every breath in or out. Then the shrapnel shells started whistling towards our trench. Soon after, into our trench. No sooner had the German artillery corrected their aim than they started in with the high explosives as well. One coal box fell into the next bay, and I was content not to see too clearly what was thrown into the air with the blast. Where in mercy's name were *our* guns? Where was Horny with his 18-pounder?

As my useless rifle dropped from my hands and my knees wobbled under me, I heard someone give the order, "Get that man to the rear!" And, for me, the battle was over.

A hot time.

Second Ypres, as it became known, was the Canadian Expeditionary Force's first battle of the war. We were outnumbered ten to one. We were gassed. We had no respirators. We were observed by airborne artillery spotters. We had no air support. We were shelled. We had no steel helmets, not till the following year. We had no artillery to fire shells at our tormentors, for our guns had been positioned out of range. Company after company of our battalion were shot to pieces in a perfect deluge of machine gun and rifle bullets, each rifle capable of rapid fire. Our country had issued us rifles that jammed if there was any dirt about or if you tried to fire more than one or two rounds a minute. Our few Colt machine guns often jammed as well. Our trenches didn't protect us, and the lower we crouched in them, the more certain we were to succumb to the gas.

And yet, defenceless as we were, we were tied into those trenches by our orders, by all the inspiring speeches we had had to endure about standing fast, by our own deadly sense of honour.

I was glad to get out, but I wasn't proud of it. How could I be when so many better men stood fast till they were killed or, ammunition exhausted, taken prisoner? I had no idea why I was permitted to escape, but one thing was certain: I wanted to know what it felt like to be a warrior instead of a punching bag. I'd got out, but I wasn't about to go home. Or into a soft Blighty posting for war cripples. In a week,

I'd stopped coughing, and after a couple more I managed to convince a medical officer that my scarred lungs were sound enough to let me return to the line. Later that year, as soon as they began calling for volunteers for trench raids, and from then till the Armistice, I was always the first to step forward, because I was determined to take the war to the enemy, whatever the risk, rather than meekly wait my turn for the chopper. Better to die like a wolf than like a lamb.

To my surprise, the war ended, and I still wasn't dead. In 1913, I'd quit the police to attend university, and had completed one year before enlisting, but on being discharged, I didn't feel settled enough to return to either patrol work or study. After the unsatisfactory call I paid on the Ingersolls, I went out west. I worked on a railway, in a lumber camp—tried my hand at prospecting—spent a few weeks fighting fires. I had the idea I'd like to fly, but never saved enough money for the lessons.

I didn't gamble, not for stakes of any size, and by the standards of the men I worked beside, drank only moderately. Most of my pay went on women. A week in Winnipeg, a weekend in Calgary with a Betty or a Lottie or a Meg. The swing of their hair, the tender softness of their skin, the smooth sweet curves of their cheeks, breasts, hips—I've sometimes thought it's a privilege just to tread the same earth with such miraculous creatures as girls, and that no price is too high to pay for their company.

"Just another irresponsible ex-serviceman," you'll say. "Fancies he has some kind of free pass to indulge himself—a lifetime exemption from normal standards of conduct. Thinks he's entitled to anything that will help him forget what he saw on the Western Front."

Not quite. Things I saw—even sights as gruesome as Horny's wound—I might have lived with. What most often induced me to buy oblivion in women's arms was something I did.

Yes, there were proud moments. In one raid on the German trenches before Vimy, I brought in three prisoners single-handed and earned my commission. But the raid before that was less glorious.

Three of us went out on a moonless night, got through the wire, and dropped into what we believed was Fritz's trench. But where was he? We couldn't see farther than two feet. The three of us fanned out. Then from somewhere a flare went up, and that blinded me worse than before. Scared me too, for it might have shown the enemy we were inside his defences. One shape came pelting around a corner from my right and impaled himself on my bayonet. I twisted it for good measure as he went down, then braced my foot against his chest while I pulled the blade out. It didn't come easily: he seemed to be grabbing at it with both hands, holding it in so he wouldn't bleed to death. Meanwhile, I felt someone coming up behind me. Without the bayonet, how was I going to deal with him? I snatched up the German's rifle. There was no time to turn it around, for over my shoulder I glimpsed steel rushing at me. I drove the Mauser butt into the other man's face and, as he went down, scrambled out of the trench and back through the gap we'd made in the wire.

Two of the three of us got back to our own lines, but a private called Fazackerley—a post office clerk on civvy street—didn't show up. While no one blamed me, I wondered if he might have been the man I struck in the dark. Had my blow with that German rifle butt snapped his neck and killed him? I confessed my fears to no one.

Later, we heard Private Fazackerley had been taken prisoner. When I got home to Canada in 1919, part of me wanted to know if Fazackerley had made it through the war, and part of me was too scared to inquire. Nearly one Canadian prisoner in ten had died in captivity. That statistic is what I was running from during those months out west.

Then, on Armistice Day in 1920, I happened to be in Vancouver. I wasn't about to march in any veterans' parade, but when all the fire hall bells in town rang out at eleven a.m., I found myself in front of Municipal Hall at 43rd and Fraser, where the ladies' auxiliary of the G.W.V.A. had erected a temporary cenotaph. Skid row bums rubbed shoulders with men in business suits and kept a respectful distance from grey-haired mothers still in mourning for their sons. A two minutes' silence was observed. The Last Post was played, snatches of poetry read.

They shall grow not old, as we that are left grow old:
Age shall not weary them, nor the years condemn.
At the going down of the sun and in the morning
We will remember them.

Growing old didn't seem such a bad thing at the time. I was reminded of Fazackerley and was sorry I'd come. As I turned to go, there he was.

"Sergeant Shenstone! I must say it's easier to recognize you when it's day, and you don't have a German rifle in your hand."

Fazackerley was a raw-boned man with a slouch and pale eyes, just as I'd remembered him. What was new was the lines in his face, a gold tooth, and a well-cut three-piece suit. I gulped hard and offered to stand him a bite to eat. At the C.P.R. Hotel Vancouver. It was the most money I had ever spent for a meal with no woman present, but he looked as if he wouldn't be used to the lunch counter at Kresge's.

"Look, I'm sorry I hit you," I said.

"Best thing that could have happened to me," Fazackerley

assured me. "I hated those trench raids, dreaded them. Frankly, sergeant, I think you saved my life."

"Don't call me sergeant, please." I didn't tell him I'd left the army a second lieutenant. "Call me son-of-a-bitch if you like. I'm sure Fritz's cage wasn't the most fun you ever had in your life."

"I'm not pretending it was. But I only had a year and a half of it. And the proof I'm not bitter is I'm working for a German shipping company now."

"Tell me, though. When you were first taken prisoner, didn't you think: 'Just wait till the war ends; I'm going to have words with that Shenstone.'"

"Of course—what do you take me for?"

His story came out over the grilled salmon. The worst part, according to Fazackerley, had been the train trip back to Germany.

"There must have been fifty of us in that pigsty of a boxcar without a vent hole anywhere. In the three days we were in there, we got three drinks of water—yep, three—and no food. Of course, my face was so swollen I couldn't have done much chewing anyway. I didn't think this POW business was up my alley at all, and I heartily wished you in a place twice as bad... Then I got lucky. When they finally unloaded us, German 'labour coordinators' tried to find out what jobs we were suited for. Some of our boys figured to get out of work by claiming to have no usable skills at all. Carpenters pretended they'd been barkeeps. Factory workers tried to pass themselves off as insurance salesmen. They all got sent to the mines. So I went a different route. I said I was an agricultural labourer, thinking to get close to the food. I'd been on a farm maybe once in my life. They bought it, though. And next I knew they'd set me planting cabbages. Then the Red Cross food parcels started coming too, and in three weeks—not even three—I was drinking Paul Shenstone's health in ersatz coffee."

My idea of punishing the man behind Peerless Armaments had lasted longer than that, but from the night we lost Fazackerley to the Germans it started to fade, and on that November 11 in 1920 it almost disappeared. My negligence could have killed one of my men. I had done nothing to earn a happy ending.

A week later, I returned to Toronto. Not everyone who resigns from the police gets welcomed back; at the time I reapplied, however, Prohibition and the difficulty of enforcing it meant more cops were needed—and, for any government job, returned servicemen were still being given the inside track. My military record and my year at college meant rapid advancement from uniformed constable to plainclothesman, and then to detective sergeant. Sergeant again after all.

I've never told this story before. I think I'd have tried to spill it to Edith, that afternoon of April 21, 1926, if we could have taken our lemonades off to a quiet corner of the Watts' living room and had an hour together undisturbed. She thought my experience with trench raids made me more likely to shoot her father. In fact, that experience made it impossible for me to do so.

If I had spoken to her, I'd have had to count on the Fazackerley rigmarole getting her off the subject of my alibi. At the time of Digby Watt's murder, I was humping May for all I was worth. My only witness: a chemical blonde with a criminal record.

Chapter Eighteen

Knocking on my apartment door woke me early on the morning after Ivan's arrest. Eight o'clock would not have been early to pick up a phone, but I had none and had to show a face that was far from ready.

"Can you cook eggs, Ned?" I asked when I saw who it was.

Cruickshank didn't deny it, so I led the way into my kitchen.

"You cook the eggs; I'll make the coffee. Or is it urgent?"

"Possibly, sergeant. A woman called Marie Burgess phoned HQ this morning. She claims to have been confidential secretary to Digby and Morris Watt."

"Yes, I know who you mean. Pince-nez. Looks like Woodrow Wilson." I pushed butter, pepper and eggs in Cruickshank's direction. "Scrambled's fine."

The frying pan was on top of the electric range. Cruickshank dropped in a frugal lump of butter and turned on the element.

"Well, I didn't actually see her. She phoned."

"And said she'd been fired?"

"Resigned, in fact. And also that Morris Watt did not get on well with his father."

I yawned. As usual, I measured coffee and water with a sleep-bleared eye. I never much liked my own coffee. Too late, I wished I'd divvied up the breakfast preparation the other way.

"Very forthcoming of her," I said. I guess it didn't really

surprise me that Morris hadn't had the gumption to give her her walking papers. "Anything else?"

"Yes, sir." Cruickshank had located a three-day-old half loaf of bread and was using considerable muscle to get it separated into slices. "She said that yesterday she found a pistol in Morris Watt's desk."

"What kind? Revolver or automatic?"

"She wasn't able to say," Cruickshank replied.

"The gun we want is only four and a half inches. She must have noticed if it was much longer than that."

"She wasn't able to say."

"Think she saw a gun at all?"

"Don't know, sir. But she claims to have a recording in which Morris Watt threatens some action against his father just two weeks before the murder. The inspector sent a car to bring her and the wax cylinder to HQ."

"Threatening his father?" I said. "I'll believe that when I hear it."

"Not a direct threat. Apparently Morris is in conversation with his wife. Digby Watt was out of the building at the time."

"Does the Burgess woman explain why, if what sonny boy says is so incriminating, he made a recording of it?"

"She says he didn't mean to. Unknown to him, the intercom mike from his office to the reception was open. When Miss Burgess heard how he was talking, she flicked the record switch on the attached Dictaphone."

The open line squared with what Morris had told me. Two weeks before his father's death, he hadn't known the switch was defective and might indeed have spoken unguardedly.

"I'll get dressed," I said.

I shaved as well. Cruickshank's eggs were still not rubbery by the time I ate them standing up. I poured a cup of coffee down my throat without having to taste it, and took the stale bread along to make a mess with on the streetcar. The motorcycle had no passenger seat, and Cruickshank had no car.

"Get anything more out of MacAllister, Ned?" I asked on the way downtown.

"He didn't say anything last night. I guess you'll want to read his article, though. He must have filed it yesterday afternoon before we picked him up. I brought along a copy of today's *Examiner*."

I wiped my hands on my trousers and reached for the paper. Ivan had written that the Watts were unhappy with police progress on the murder investigation. The flapper daughter Edith was playing private detective. Questions were being raised about Detective Sergeant Paul Shenstone's fitness to handle the case.

"Biting as a toothless mouse," I remarked. "Milder than what he would send his paper this morning if given the chance."

Marie Burgess was in Sanderson's office when we arrived. Her face behind her pince-nez wore a smug, dutiful expression. Every last steel-coloured wisp of her hair was pulled into a tight bun. She wasn't a woman that went in for perfume. Around her in the close room, there wafted rather a scent of Listerine. If she uses that much, I thought, it's because she's a secret drinker. An entertaining thought. I wondered if the inspector, who was courteously not belching pipe smoke for once, had reached the same conclusion. The day was young, but already he looked tired. He sat in his usual place, Marie Burgess in the chair opposite, with a Dictaphone on the desk between them. Ned and I stood.

"Everyone have enough room?" asked the inspector, insisting on his little joke. "Miss Burgess has just been explaining the microphone malfunction that allowed this recording to be made, a defect she says Mr. Morris Watt was unaware of at the time."

Sanderson had already listened to the cylinder and even had Lindstrom type up a transcript, but played the recording again so I could identify the speaker. It was Morris's voice all right, raw and emphatic, alternating with the calmer tones of a woman that might have been Lavinia—though she was farther from the mike and none of us could make out what she said. According to the Burgess woman, Mrs. Morris Watt had dropped by the office while downtown shopping.

To my ears, it sounded as if after year on docile year of self-denial, Morris had blown his cork, not angrily but desperately, because there was just nowhere else for the pressure to go.

Morris: I wish he would retire, but he won't as long as he has breath.

Lavinia inaudible.

Morris: I'll give Dad another two weeks and see. Till the week of the nineteenth. Then, if there's no position for me, I'll do it. I'll do it, cost what it costs.

Lavinia inaudible.

Morris: It won't hurt him as much as you think. I'll make it as painless as I can.

After that, both speakers were too far from the microphone to be understood.

"Inspector Sanderson," I said, "would you mind if I asked Miss Burgess a question or two?"

"I suggest you do. Miss Burgess, I believe you've met Detective Sergeant Shenstone."

She didn't say she had or hadn't, but swivelled in her chair and tilted her long head back to give me a better view of her candid, co-operative face.

"Miss Burgess, did you make a note of the exact date of this conversation?"

"I wrote it on the cylinder box." The cardboard box was on the desk. She picked it up and read, "Conversation between Mr. and Mrs. Morris Watt, 4:20 p.m., April 4, 1926."

"So the nineteenth Mr. Morris Watt refers to would have been the nineteenth of this month, last Monday—the eve of his father's death?"

"Yes, that's right."

"Good. Now did you hear any part of the conversation that isn't on this cylinder?"

"Well, yes. Before the words that are there, I heard Mr. Morris raise his voice, which was not at all usual for him. He said he wouldn't stand for the way his father was treating him. It sounded serious, so it seemed to me I'd better record it. That's when I turned on the machine."

"Was there anything else you heard, Miss Burgess? Anything that would clarify the *it* that Morris Watt was going to do, the *it* he would make as painless as possible?"

"No, sir."

"After you made this recording, did you seek clarification from Morris Watt as to what this *it* might be?"

"No, sir, I certainly didn't."

"Did you advise Morris Watt that the switch on his console had a tendency to stick and that when it stuck you could hear whatever he said at his desk?"

"No, sir. I thought I'd better wait and see if there were further developments. I mean, further conversations along the same lines."

"And were there?"

"No."

"Did you make any other recordings?"

"None."

"Did you at any time reveal the existence of this recording to either Morris or Digby Watt?"

"I did not. Frankly, once I'd made it, it didn't seem to amount to much. And I knew Mr. Digby Watt wouldn't approve of my making it. He had very high moral ideals. Sometimes gentlemen of his quality need someone to watch out for them. But, as I say, I came to think there was nothing in it."

"You didn't believe the word *it* referred to killing Digby Watt?"

"No, not until yesterday when I saw the gun in Mr. Morris Watt's drawer. Until then I simply couldn't imagine him connected with any sort of violence. That's why I didn't come forward with this wax cylinder any earlier."

"Thank you, Miss Burgess. You've answered all my questions very precisely and forthrightly. Now I'd like you to be just as precise and forthright in describing this gun you saw in Morris Watt's desk drawer. Was it, for example, longer than that Dictaphone cylinder?"

"I couldn't say, sir. Guns frighten me, so I closed the drawer before I got a proper look."

"You don't strike me, Miss Burgess, as someone that frightens easily—"

But Sanderson cut me off.

"We've shown Miss Burgess various guns, sergeant, and she hasn't been able to narrow the field. For my part, whatever pistol Morris Watt has in his desk, I want it looked into. The sooner the better. Take Acting Detective Cruickshank and get yourselves over to 96 Adelaide Street West."

I picked up a carbon of the transcript from Lindstrom's desk on the way out, but once again didn't bother taking my service revolver. Cruickshank followed me to the door.

"Stay here, Ned," I told him. "Never mind the inspector.

I'll follow this up, and you go see whether a night in custody has loosened Ivan's tongue any."

"Sure you don't need help?"

"With Morris?" I threw him a sidelong glance.

I greeted the elevator operator at 96 Adelaide West by name and asked for the fourth floor. Instead of being pinned up as before, Harold's right sleeve hung down full and a glove had been pulled on over an artificial hand. A hand more for show than for use, though, as he still reached across and worked the controls with his left. If he had yielded to Digby Watt's offers, he would have been given a more useful model. I brooded on that for a bit. Yet I could see that the inexpensive prosthesis was Harold's independent way of paying tribute to his late employer and friend.

"You're the detective, aren't you, sir?" said Harold. "Are you close to making an arrest?"

"Very close."

There was no one else in the elevator car, but still Harold dropped his voice to a more confidential level.

"Do you think the killer might strike again, sir, the way the paper is saying? I mean, shouldn't Mr. Morris Watt have some protection?"

"We've no reason to think he's in danger, Harold, but I'll keep your suggestion in mind."

On the fourth floor, a new woman sat behind the desk opposite the elevators. She was young and strongly built, with the look of a golfer, and she was typing at a terrifying rate. When I identified myself and asked for Morris Watt, she smiled pleasantly and said he was on the phone, if Mr. Shenstone would be good enough to wait.

"Certainly," I said. "And after he gets off the phone, you'll be holding his calls till I'm finished speaking to him."

Her unplucked eyebrows went up, and her smile

acquired the extra twinkle that said she thought I had some nerve.

"I'll tell him you said so."

She didn't have to. Morris had the same idea.

This time I was shown into the other office, the one that had been Digby Watt's. The premises were only slightly larger than those Morris had previously occupied, and his tenure was doubtless no more than provisional till the board of directors had met to settle on the succession. Still, it must have been satisfying to sit for once in Daddy's chair.

Morris Watt did not rise. He sat with hands folded on his father's desk and a look of dignified mistrust on his photogenic face.

"Mr. Watt," I began, "do you continue to maintain you have no pistol in your possession?"

Without a word, Morris Watt opened a drawer and took out a hefty, blue-grey metal revolver, which he laid—butt-end towards me—on the desk.

"No," I said, "the gun isn't enough: I'll need a statement. Is it yours? Did you discover it here? How long have you had it?"

"Two days ago, sergeant, when you last came to Dominion Consolidated Holdings, I had never seen this pistol. I give you my word on that."

"Tell me more."

"I suppose you heard about this from Marie Burgess. She resigned her post yesterday, all the time pretending she was being forced out. I guess grief takes us all differently."

"The gun, Mr. Watt."

"The two important things about the gun are that I did not lie to you about it and that its calibre is too large for it to have been the gun that killed my father."

I came to the desk and picked up the revolver, a Webley

Mark VI. Virtually identical to the one I had carried during the last year of the war. With a calibre of .455, these rugged darlings discharged with a kick that made them worse than useless in the hands of anyone without long training. The cylinder contained five bullets. I shoved the six-inch barrel into the waistband of my trousers and felt hard-boiled.

"I'll decide what's important, sir. You decide whether you want to talk to me here or in an interrogation room at headquarters."

I was leaning over the desk, and Morris Watt had to tilt his head back to meet my eyes. Even if it had been a better posture for looking down one's nose, Morris Watt was too fundamentally civil to make an impressive job of it.

"You're trying to protect someone," I said. "Needlessly. As you say, this isn't the murder weapon. I still want to know where it came from."

"I bought it for self-defence. After father was killed that way, I thought anything could happen."

"It's Harold's, isn't it? Either he told you he had armed himself for your protection or you saw the bulge under his jacket. Lift jockeys' rigs are tight-fitting, and this is a bulky gun. Don't worry. I'm not going to make trouble for him."

Morris looked down at his folded hands. Seeing, perhaps, what uphill work it would be to make them pass as wielders of such a cannon.

"I was afraid someone would get hurt," he said. "Actually, I was afraid *he* would get hurt—so I persuaded him to let me have it. I was going to hand it over to the police for destruction. I never feel safer with firearms around."

"I'm inclined to believe you. Yesterday evening, when you got a note from Curtis to the effect that I had been brandishing a .25 automatic, you rushed me off your property as fast as you could, and told him to stay out of sight while you were doing it."

Morris Watt passed his hand over the lower part of his face, remembering the danger he had fancied his family had been in.

"I spoke to your inspector last night," he said, "and asked, in view of your connection with my father through Peerless Armaments, that another detective investigate his murder. Do you know what he said? He said he could give me another detective or he could have the case wrapped up today, but not both. Will you wrap it up today, sergeant?"

"Possibly. There's something about the timing that bothers me, though. You found your father dead at a time you estimate to be two fifteen or a little later?"

"Yes."

"And the journalist Ivan MacAllister was already on the scene?"

"Yes."

"Are you sure you saw your father alive as late as two a.m.?"

"As I told you, I didn't check my watch at the moment I left him, but it must have been between 1:55 and 2:05."

"The problem with that, Mr. Watt, is that Ivan MacAllister was summoned to the scene by a phone call made around a quarter to two. Presumably by your father's murderer. Except that, on your account, at a quarter to two your father was still alive. How did the caller know that by the time MacAllister arrived, he would find Digby Watt dead?"

"I don't know," said Morris.

"I can think of one explanation," I said. "And remember it is no more my wish to be assigned to this case than it is yours to have me. That one explanation is that you shot your father before you made that call to MacAllister. Then you could have gone to the garage and tampered with the car and made sure you didn't return to the scene till MacAllister had found the body."

I braced myself for Morris's excited protestations of love for his father and of indignation at my suggestion. Everything I might have heard in the first hours of his bereavement. Today, however, his surprising response was to reason with me.

"Really, sergeant. I don't know enough about cars to have sabotaged the Gray-Dort. And I didn't call MacAllister: he would have recognized my voice when I met him on the street."

"You acted hysterical when you spoke to him on the street. Your voice was completely different from normal."

"Rot!" Now Morris was getting gratifyingly heated. "Utter nonsense. But let him hear my 'normal' voice, if you like. You can bring him here and ask him if I made that call."

"I just might," I bluffed. Tinker would be the one who would have to identify the murderer's voice, and Tinker's hearing was questionable. I changed my ground. "I've always found it odd that when you came home that morning and Miss Watt asked you who'd shot your father, you didn't say you didn't know. You said that would be for the police to find out."

"What I meant was I didn't think we should be speculating as to the killer's identity. I wanted the matter handled professionally... Well, *I* certainly didn't shoot Dad. Why would I?"

"Why?" I said, letting it be heard how little the word impressed me. "The psychologists have plenty to say about sons' hating fathers—but let's leave Freud out of it and look at your circumstances in particular. If my dad had kept me down the way yours did you, and I hadn't felt able to go off on my own, I would have wanted him dead. On April 4, you told your wife you would give your father until this week to find a position for you or else you'd do it, 'cost what it costs'."

Morris blinked.

"Oh," he said at last. "The broken intercom. Marie Burgess again. But I only meant that I would take a job somewhere else, even at considerable financial sacrifice. A job where I'd have something to contribute."

"Easily said," I continued, "but I'm not done. Suppose you found out about the bad shells before Edith unearthed Robert Taylor's letter. You were enough of a soldier to feel the betrayal of those boys your father killed. And, to cap it off, maybe you discovered the real reason that Olive stopped wanting to see Digby Watt. You had motives enough. And all your air of decency and professed dislike of firearms would give you enough protective cover."

While delivering this speech, I sauntered towards the window, deliberately leaving my back as a target for Morris. The murder weapon had still not been found. Would it not be sweet if, by turning just in time, I found it in Morris's hand?

The office was quiet.

I gazed down through the window, giving my host a little more time. I gazed down at a phone booth. This was the side street, Sheppard Street. And suddenly I saw it. This was how the murderer had known when to phone MacAllister's apartment. He had studied Digby Watt's routine, had identified which window belonged to his office, knew how many minutes would elapse from the time the light in this window went off to the time when Digby Watt would emerge from the brass doors on

Adelaide Street West. You could watch for the light to go off from the street or from one of the windows of the building opposite. For example, behind the phone booth was a newsagent's shop.

I had forgotten all about Morris and jumped when I heard Morris's voice, no longer heated in the least, mild as milk.

"I wish I *had* known about the bad shells before yesterday. I'd like to do something about that poor man Horner Ingersoll, sergeant, if you could put me in touch with his family."

"Now's not the moment," I said as I rushed from the room.

I pushed the button for the elevator, didn't wait, and plunged into the stairwell. On Adelaide Street, the climbing sun was still struggling to peep over the office towers. The sidewalk was not crowded, but seemed so to my impatience. I trotted briskly around the corner, crossed the street, entered the newsagent's. There was no bell on the door, but the shop was small, and Arthur Ingersoll looked up from making change for a woman buying the latest *Screenland*. The light was behind me, and I was sure I wasn't recognized. We hadn't seen each other since 1919. Seven years. Ingersoll had been ill then. His hair now was even thinner, and his tendons stood out even more, but there was no lethargy about him, no sluggishness. His movements were quick and watchful.

"Help you?" he barked irritably in my direction.

I waited for the customer to leave. This brown and dusty little shop was clearly a step or more down from the concession at the King Edward Hotel. No international newspapers were sold. The cigar case held only domestic brands. A curtained opening behind the counter would lead to a none too generous storage area behind a flimsy partition.

The young office worker with the movie magazine cast me a questioning look from under the low rim of her cloche hat as she passed. The door fell to behind her.

"Yes," said Arthur Ingersoll. "What do you want?"

"When did you last speak to Ivan MacAllister?"

"MacAllister writes for the *Examiner*. There's the stand. It's two cents."

I turned the sign on the shop door from OPEN to CLOSED.

"He told you what happened to Horny," I said, "didn't he? What really happened."

"Get out of my shop." Arthur Ingersoll was plainly itching to come out from behind his counter to take a closer look and maybe a poke at me, but something was holding him back. "Go on, clear out. Now."

"And you found," I went on, noticing how the voice of command that had once left me so cowed still had considerable bite, "you found that you'd been blaming Germans all these years for what was really the fault of Canadians. Most particularly, Digby Watt. The same Digby Watt whose big fat office tower you have to look at every day through your grubby little shop front. The same Digby Watt whose enterprises kept prospering as yours were failing."

"Who are you?"

"Someone you've known a long time. Mostly, of course, I had nothing to say—but once I did. If you'd listened then, it might have saved your neck."

"Paul? I won't have you shutting down my business."

"You're through with business, sir, and you know it. You knew it the night of the twentieth when you plugged Horny's killer. You wanted to get caught, didn't you? You dialled MacAllister's number, even though MacAllister might have recognized your voice. You left the shell casings at the scene."

Chin raised, Ingersoll tried one of his silencing silences.

"And," I went on, "you're keeping the gun behind the counter there, when if you had wanted to commit the perfect murder, you would have thrown it away."

"I don't know why Horny ever bothered with you. You showed nothing like his ginger. Horny—why, he had the girls lining up—"

"I carried Horny to the dressing station, Mr. Ingersoll. It was my hand he hung onto when he died."

"Then why didn't you tell me about it? Why didn't you tell me about that shell?"

"Believe me, I tried. But you preferred the officer's fairy tale. I came to your house seven years ago prepared to tell you all about Peerless Armaments."

"Then to hell with Digby Watt! What's Digby Watt to you, Paul—apart from the bastard that blew your friend to kingdom come?"

"So you killed him."

"I'm not saying that."

"Let me tell it then," I said. "After phoning MacAllister's, you waited on the corner till you saw the two Watts come outside. When Morris went for the car, you approached Digby. You didn't shoot him right away, though. If you had, you would have been facing the building, and the cartridge cases would have been ejected behind you into Adelaide Street. Watt would have fallen with his head the other way. So you must have had words with him, maybe introduced yourself. When he saw the gun in your hand, he backed away towards the street. You fired three times, and he fell. The empty shells bounced back off the building. Then you undid his fly and pulled his privates out, just to let the world know what this killing was about. Too bad you didn't have more time. You might have got really creative."

"Digby Watt didn't deserve to live."

"Do you?" I pulled Harold's heavy revolver from my waistband and, without actually aiming at Arthur Ingersoll, made sure he saw it. I held it broadside, with the barrel pointing towards the ceiling.

Ingersoll's hand—wrapped around a pocket pistol—appeared instantly above the counter. The action was so quick that, ready as I was, I was almost too late. I threw Harold's gun, all thirty-eight ounces of it, forcefully into Ingersoll's face. Ingersoll's arm swung wide of me as the semiautomatic went off and a .25 slug lodged in the panelling.

I leaped and rolled over the counter, scattering displays of cough drops and pipe cleaners. I rolled into Ingersoll before he could recover his aim. Now I had to get that gun. For a chilling instant, I found myself staring into the muzzle's dark eye. But already I was also grasping the top slide and pushing it back. Before it could be discharged, the cartridge was dragged from the barrel and jammed in the breech; my hand over the aperture meanwhile prevented ejection of the round. This with my right, which meant my back was to Ingersoll. My left hand was kept busy parrying some fiery punches to the kidneys from Ingersoll's left. The narrow space, however, was not conducive to a display of boxing talent.

With the gun jammed—and useless as anything more than a club—we came to grips in earnest. I spun around to face Ingersoll, twisting his right arm in the process. The strong, silent man's cry of pain was so loud I couldn't hear whether any bones cracked. I was just starting to consider the battle won when Ingersoll's knee slammed up into my crotch. True to form, I thought. Before he could get both feet back on the floor, I overbalanced him and pinned him to the linoleum.

I was all over him now, straddling his chest, gripping his upper arms so tightly his fingers must have tingled. I could hear the jammed pistol slip from his grasp. I had a good look down into eyes I'd known all my life. The angle I saw them from was unfamiliar, but I can't say the hate that filled them altogether was. I thought how Horny's dad, he-man champion of artillery and big guns, should have resorted to such a very small one. Perhaps he read my mind. Anger tightened the skin on his forehead till I thought it might rip open. He had no way left of striking me. So he spat. The lump of phlegm lacked the force to reach my face and fell wetly onto his brown shirt front. He didn't try anything more.

The shop door opened, and presently Ned Cruickshank's rosy face was peering anxiously over the counter.

"I don't like to interfere, sergeant, but would a pair of handcuffs be of any use to you?"

"Shouldn't be necessary, Ned." I dug out my wallet badge and held it above my captive's face. "Arthur Ingersoll," I said, "in the name of the king, I arrest you for the murder of Digby Watt."

Having started one of his sulks, Arthur Ingersoll said nothing.

Epilogue

Detective Sergeant Paul Shenstone?"

A throaty purr over the office phone, but classy. I wondered if I knew any women like that.

"Who wants me?"

"It's Lavinia Watt, Mr. Shenstone. Edith and I were wondering if we could invite you to tea on the Twenty-fourth of May holiday."

"What's the occasion, Mrs. Watt?" I didn't think the Glen Road ladies had pegged me for a special admirer of the old queen.

"We feel you were treated rather badly last time you were over at the house."

That would be the evening Morris gave me the bum's rush.

"So you'd like the chance to do it again?"

Lavinia's laugh was more polite than a guffaw, heartier than a titter.

"No-o. But I suppose there is a condition of a sort. Is the month that has passed since Arthur Ingersoll's arrest time enough that you feel you can discuss the case?"

"Up to a point."

"Then consider yourself welcome 'up to a point' at three thirty, Victoria Day."

I wasn't on duty that day, so I decided to go. I even got my suit dry-cleaned, which must have been a shock for it. I washed and ironed my newest shirt and tightened my tie well past the point at which it was comfortable. I didn't take them flowers, as we'd be sitting in a greenhouse. I didn't take them anything. I wasn't courting, after all.

There was no answer at first to my ring, so I tried knocking as well, and wondered if they had changed their minds. Eventually, Mrs. Hubbard opened the door.

"Yes, there's the policeman. Nothing wrong with the bell. I just don't step as quick as Nita, and she has the day off." The portly housekeeper adjusted her bifocals. "Don't you look spruce!"

"Hello, Mrs. H." I felt a smile break out on my face before I could think to put it there. "How have you been?"

"Oh, I suppose we're getting adjusted. I will admit I still have teary times when I think of Mr. Watt and how he just missed seeing his first grandchild."

"A pity for him, but glad news for the family."

"I hope I haven't said more than I should have."

"Of course not. You can keep it under my hat." I handed it to her. "Are they in the conservatory? I know my way."

The Watt women wore short, light spring dresses—Lavinia's daffodil yellow, Edith's virginal white—with stockings to match. Their blonde and dark heads were huddled over the *Toronto Examiner*, apparently the real estate ads. Lavinia was first to notice I'd arrived. She actually stood up. Primed by Mrs. Hubbard, I noticed the incipient bulge at her waist.

"Mr. Shenstone, how good of you to let us have part of your holiday!"

"My pleasure, Mrs. Watt. Is it not a day off for your husband?"

"Unfortunately not. Morris has just started a new job." I could hear this change didn't exactly thrill her.

Edith, who had remained immersed in her reading,

looked up at last. Once they were on you, those eyes of blue fire made having been ignored worth it.

"With the Y.M.C.A.," she said, "work much better suited to his temperament than Dominion Consolidated Holdings."

I remembered Marie Burgess's eavesdropping and Morris's explanation of what he had meant by doing *it.* Now he'd done it. I wished him well.

"And he's also dead set on selling the house." Lavinia sank back down into her well-cushioned wicker chair, indolently waving me into one only just less upholstered. "Please don't tell the servants, Mr. Shenstone. It would only upset them."

Solid footsteps in the hall announced the arrival of Mrs. Hubbard with the tea and scones. Big scones—she must have known anything too dainty would make me ill at ease.

"I believe Lavinia has warned you," said Edith when everyone had been served, "that this is not strictly a social occasion. We intend to pump you unmercifully."

"I'd like to know why Arthur Ingersoll killed Father," Lavinia sighed. "Such a sweet man, a kind man—I still can't imagine why anyone would want to take his life."

"It had to be because Peerless made the shell that killed his son," said Edith. "The why is clear, but how did Arthur Ingersoll know about the shell? Morris said the families were never told their sons died of bad Canadian munitions rather than good German ones."

"Good?" Lavinia made a moue.

I grinned to show I knew what she meant.

"He knew," I said, "because in February, Ivan MacAllister finally told him. No one told him sooner because he didn't want to hear, and what good could it do him anyway? I tried to talk to him about it in 1919 and didn't get very far. MacAllister didn't even try, not then, though he knew who Ingersoll was. Horner Ingersoll had talked about his dad's concession at the King Edward Hotel. MacAllister worked downtown and was always buying smokes or magazines, so he knew Ingersoll by sight."

"What changed MacAllister's mind about telling Ingersoll?" asked Edith.

"In a word, Ingersoll's bigotry. Do you two remember how you felt about Germans during the war?"

"I don't recall," said Lavinia. "I'm sure I was too young to feel anything."

"I hated them in a ten-year-old way," said Edith. "Meaning I had no idea what a German was—or what hate was, for that matter."

"That's what was wanted during those years. Keep hating, keep making sacrifices for the cause. I'm not saying we shouldn't have gone to war. The Germans were aggressors and no mistake. But the venom seemed to increase in potency the farther you got from the fighting. Those of us at the front didn't love Fritz, but we knew the soldiers we faced had no more decided to invade Belgium than we had. Now Ingersoll, on the other hand, got this letter from his son's lieutenant. A letter saying his son's butchers would be shown no mercy. A word like butcher just slid off the officer's pen, but it didn't slip out of Arthur Ingersoll's mind. An idiotic word to have written, even if the lieutenant's story had been true. The German gunners were no more butchers than was his own son or Ivan MacAllister or Robert Taylor. But the lieutenant called them butchers and swore Horner Ingersoll would be avenged. 'Take up our quarrel with the foe,' Arthur Ingersoll heard his son say. 'If ye break faith with us who die we shall not sleep.' And then Ingersoll saw Germany beaten and get a soft peace, a gutless peace. The bigwigs had broken faith with the men they sent into battle."

"You sound as if you're not just speaking from Arthur Ingersoll's point of view," said Edith.

"As regards the peace treaty, I can see his point. But he didn't *see* that point; he lived with it twisting and turning in his gut because he had lost his son, his first-born."

"Please stop," Lavinia begged.

"I'm sorry," I said. "Let me just say that Arthur Ingersoll did not sign on to the Treaty of Versailles. He continued to wage his own guerrilla war against the German people. But not really the German people, who were too far away. He waged war on anyone he met with a German accent or a German name. He lost his concession at the King Edward Hotel after a complaint against him by a Swiss manufacturer. In his next shop on Sheppard Street, his opportunities were more limited, but he still had his apartments to rent out, and it gave him great pleasure to tell tenants those apartments weren't for them, or maybe to let them rent and then throw them out in the middle of winter. There weren't enough Germans to absorb his animosity, so he took exception to foreigners in general, any one of whom might have come from the former Austro-Hungarian Empire. Are you with me so far?"

Nodding blonde and dark heads. A hum of assent.

"Now, here's where MacAllister comes into the picture. One day, he's in the Sheppard Street shop, and he hears Ingersoll chewing out some poor Schmidt or Mueller. MacAllister killed his share of Germans, but that was wartime, and now he has a German landlord. So he puts Ingersoll wise."

"Did Ingersoll believe him?" asked Edith. "I mean, after seven years, his mind was so set. He had his villains all picked out."

"And he still despises foreigners to this day. Bit by bit, however, he stopped blaming them. Once it sunk in that MacAllister was telling the truth, Ingersoll had a new villain. And his rage against your father was all the greater because he had been lied to. His rage was all the greater because he had been led to persecute not just innocent individuals—he'd never cared about that—but individuals from the wrong category altogether. Why should he have had a worse conscience about the latter than the former? You tell me. All I know is that he wanted to make Digby Watt pay for the pain of that bad conscience, and for the pain of learning that Ingersoll's own country let his son down, and for the pain of having a far less glorious death to remember. In the corrected history, Horner Ingersoll figured not as a hero but as a chump."

"You're not sparing our feelings," said Lavinia. "Silly of me to be afraid you'd be too discreet."

"I think he is. He could have said a gelded chump."

"Edith!"

"No, Vinnie, that's important. That's why Ingersoll left Father...exposed."

"Now again," I hastened on, "I'm speaking from Arthur Ingersoll's point of view. Your father was no more guilty in 1926 than he was in 1915. In fact, he had done a great deal of good for soldiers and their families since then. But for Horner's father, *your* father was the new Satan. And it sure didn't help that your father was a business success while Ingersoll was a business mediocrity."

"I'm suddenly feeling less brave about this." Edith shivered inside her gossamer frock. "I know Ingersoll's already done his worst, but still—he must have been obsessed."

"He was. From February to April, he studied Digby

Watt's movements with fanatical care. He learned which office your father used, which window to watch, which garage the Gray-Dort was parked on top of when he worked later than eleven. He told me he thought of replacing the steering pin with a piece of soft metal that would give out under the least pressure of use—something like the metal of those shell casings."

"Morris could have been hurt," Lavinia gasped.

I stammered a little as the parts of Ingersoll's confession I was not going to tell these women flashed through my head. How, for instance, he'd at one time considered rigging the car to explode. A son for a son. But he couldn't believe losing Morris would cut Digby Watt up as much as he, Arthur Ingersoll, was cut up over Horny's death and the lies surrounding it. Nothing short of confronting Digby Watt would do—confronting him and then executing him.

"In the end," I managed to get out, "he just wanted your husband delayed. Maybe scared a little too, but principally kept out of the way so he could rant longer before shooting. It was a battle of the fathers, the prewar generation, not of the sons."

Lavinia refilled my cup, absentmindedly adding milk.

"You spoke," she said, "of the soldiers' not harbouring hard feelings after the war. That was Morris's point about ex-servicemen not being vindictive. He was right, wasn't he?"

"Partly," I replied. "Of very few people can it be said they are or are not vindictive one hundred per cent. Take Ivan MacAllister. He would never have killed Digby Watt, but he did remove the shell casings in the hopes of making a solution to the murder more difficult."

Not to mention—and I had no intention of mentioning —the trophy photograph.

"Why do you think Ingersoll left those shell casings?" said Edith.

"Carelessness," I replied. "I don't think he bothered to find out whether they could be matched to his gun—as they have been."

"But is it also possible he was asking to be arrested?"

"A great detective can't admit *that,*" Lavinia objected, evidently grateful to be able to inject a jocular note into our post mortem. "It makes his solving the mystery seem less spectacular."

"I'm only moderately vain," I rejoined, "so I can half admit it. I did accuse him of wanting to be caught, but on further reflection it seems to me this is another question where the answer lies between yes and no. The revenge killer wants to get away with it, but he also wants his deed recognized. What Ingersoll most required was for your father to die, but that death would bring no joy unless the reason for it became known. Not known to everyone, perhaps, but to someone. Hence it was important that MacAllister find the body. So important that Ingersoll took the chance of phoning MacAllister before the murder even happened. MacAllister would interpret your father's murder as justice for Horner Ingersoll, even if he wasn't allowed to report it that way."

"Did MacAllister know Ingersoll was the killer?" asked Lavinia.

"He must have had his suspicions," Edith asserted.

"I agree, Miss Watt. It wasn't till after we'd arrested Ingersoll that MacAllister 'remembered' telling him about the true cause of Horner's death. But I'd be surprised if it wasn't the first thing that occurred to him when he saw your father's body."

"What will happen to him?" asked Lavinia.

Ivan's art photos had not become public knowledge or the subject of criminal charges. To my mind, he had trouble enough. I'd expended a certain amount of venom on Ivan, but from this distance I had to recognize that we had at least this much in common: the war had left us both with a stubborn thirst for justice and a shallow sense of fun.

"In view of past services to the police," I said, "he'll draw a light sentence. But of his own volition, he contributed nothing to the investigation, so he will be tried and convicted as an accessory and will have to carry a record. The *Examiner*, you'll have noticed, has already replaced him."

"Yes," said Lavinia. "The new man writes that even though Ingersoll has confessed, his lawyer is working on an insanity plea. So there's hope he may not hang."

"And you, Mr. Shenstone?"

"Still employed, thank you, Miss Watt."

"Speculation is buzzing as to why you decided to fight Arthur Ingersoll rather than just arrest him."

Talk about vindictive. Part of me had wanted to knock Arthur Ingersoll down since I was ten years old. But I didn't think I'd tell Edith that till I knew her better.

"It was quicker than obtaining a search warrant. I needed the gun to force a confession, so I goaded him into showing it."

"Morris tells me you had Harold's pistol," said Lavinia, "but you didn't fire it to defend yourself."

"A movie detective would have, wouldn't he?" I said. "I wasn't in a movie, though, and here's how I thought. First off, I wasn't going to rely for my protection on a firearm I didn't know and hadn't loaded. Another thing: if I shot Ingersoll with a gun that big, I couldn't be sure of not killing him. Then we'd never have been able to answer the questions you're asking today. What's more, the wall behind

Ingersoll was flimsy. What if Mrs. Ingersoll were on the other side? I just couldn't take the chance of a stray bullet finding her. She's quite innocent of your father's death."

"I think that's very responsible of you, Mr. Shenstone." Lavinia bestowed on me a toothy smile.

Her sister-in-law was not about to let me off so lightly.

"There was gunplay, however," said Edith. "In view of the flimsiness of the partitions, wasn't it reckless on your part to allow that?"

"Ingersoll had a smaller gun, a .25 Beretta rather than a .455 Webley, and Ingersoll's was pointed the other way. What I had to make sure of was that no bullet went through the front window into the street. If the shot went into the side wall of the shop, it would sink into the wood without ricochet and be stopped by the exterior wall of stone behind. I took a gamble, and it paid off."

"Reckless," Edith murmured—not accusingly, but as if she were trying to work something out in her own mind. "Do you like lilacs, Mr. Shenstone?"

"Are they the purple flowers that grow on trees?"

"Why don't you come and see?"

"I think if you don't mind, Edie, I'll sit here awhile longer." Lavinia picked up the paper and turned from the real estate page to an account of the fashions worn at Woodbine for the sixty-seventh running of the King's Plate. "On your way through, could you ask Mrs. Hubbard to clear the tea things?"

Edith and I went out by the French doors and strolled to the right of the hedge screening the garage. Slowly in the spring sunshine, we crossed a broad lawn towards the far border, where purple blossoms—and white ones too—weighed down the lilac bushes. My nose twitched with the anticipation of the heady feminine perfume before we were remotely within range. Except for that moment in her cottage, it was the first time I had been quite alone with Edith. I could sense her to my right, the crest of her jet-black waves of hair rising and falling at the level of my ears, her left hand swinging loose and open at her side. I felt that I should have been wearing tennis whites, that my suit was quite wrong for the setting, and that she was showing me a pointed and personal indulgence by not mentioning it.

"There's something I'd like you to do," she said.

"What?"

"You remember the night we drove to Lake Simcoe?"

"Sure."

"On the way up, Curtis told us that Olive accused my father of killing her sister. Do you remember that?"

"Yes." Perhaps I was talked out. Or made tongue-tied by Edith's closeness and the lilac bushes looming up ahead.

"I paid a call on Olive and got the whole story. She didn't want to tell it, especially not to me, but I persisted."

I nodded without turning my head.

"To me," said Edith, "it's quite clear who killed Janet Teddington, and it wasn't my father."

"If one is guilty, everyone else is innocent?"

"No. Two are guilty. I despair of finding the abortionist, but I've got the address of Billings's Garage. I'm assured there is no time limit for commencing a prosecution for rape. Can you help make sure the man's charged?"

We had reached the end of the garden. I stopped and turned towards her. She was looking up into my face.

"I can't beat a confession out of him, and the only witnesses are dead."

"I suppose you're right," she said after some internal struggle with life's unfairness.

"If you want to do some good," I suggested, "why not

make it your project to talk Nita's parents into accepting Curtis as a son-in-law?"

Edith put her hand to her throat. Her face was wearing its quizzical look.

"Maybe I shall. I'm surprised you take an interest in Curtis's happiness."

"Judging by the last time I was here? With all your talk that day of trench raids and close-quarters homicide, I thought you were trying to get me hanged."

"I just wanted to see if you'd react guiltily."

"To provoke me—as I provoked Arthur Ingersoll in his shop?"

"Well, yes."

"My technique with Curtis."

She smiled and looked back across the lawn.

"Did I, in your practised judgment, react guiltily?"

"Not at all." She faced me again abruptly. "You're laughing at me."

"Only because I think you're big enough to take it."

"I'm actually quite petty and small." She returned to surveying her rich domain, her shoulder almost touching my chest. "Unlike Lavinia, I won't cry if Ingersoll dies on the scaffold."

"Improbable," I said. "They'll bargain with him to prevent the story of the bad shells coming out. Some of the negligent manufacturers are still living and influential."

The lilac branches swayed above us, shaking down their scent. High bushes, established wealth. But the property was about to be sold. Its owner was working for the Y. Maybe I wasn't so far out of my social set, after all. I settled my hand into the small of her back. She didn't shrink from the touch.

"Dad hung his last radio antenna, his biggest, from the garage all the way over to that tree—the oak. Three days later the wind blew it down."

"And for those three days, did it improve his reception?"

"Not so you'd notice. Tell me, Paul, are you sorry Digby Watt was murdered?"

"Murder stinks. I'm sorry as anything you had to lose a father that way."

"Cut it out!" She had already wheeled out of my grasp. "It's too late in the game to palm me off with that."

I hope I looked ashamed. I felt it.

"The things I'm feeling," said Edith, "and the way you've been acting towards me have put a big decision on my plate. To make it, I need you to look me in the eye and tell me that you wish my father were alive."

To say I felt like hell would be understatement. This girl was the thing that made most sense in my world. She wasn't just beautiful. She was luminous—uniquely clear in outline and substance. Her shortcomings were the perishable ones of youth. Her loyal and forthright heart was built to last. I was thirty-four, and this was the best chance I had ever had for something big and long-term. I couldn't promise myself there'd be another like it. And the damnedest was that that bullshit answer I gave had just lengthened the odds against me. From being sorry her father had been murdered, I now had to be sorry her father was dead.

I could give it a try. I could certainly admit to myself I'd exaggerated when I told Sanderson I had no sympathy for Digby Watt. For one thing, he'd fathered Edith. Would he ever have given me a look-in with her? He had walked out with Olive. That gave me hope he was no snob. "I'm sorry your father is dead."

"A hundred per cent sorry, or is there some small part of you that thinks he got what he had coming? I have to know."

"If you'll hear me out, Edith, I'll be as straight as I can."

She was open-minded enough for that. She arched her clean black eyebrows a little higher to show she was listening.

"Yes, I went back a long way with Horner Ingersoll, but I got over his death long ago. If my feelings were all that mattered, I'd hold no grudge. But you said yourself we've no right to blot out others' pain. To kill your own soldiers in wartime, even unintentionally, is pretty bad."

"My father was not a bad man. He did more good in the world than someone like you could ever imagine. Surely he can be forgiven what was no more than an oversight."

Here was a change from the young hanging judge of a moment earlier. Mercy for Digby Watt, none for Arthur Ingersoll.

"I don't know who has the right to forgive your father. But I always heard, if you're to be forgiven, you have to admit guilt. You have to be sorry and try to make things right."

"Have you forgotten the papers I found in Dad's desk?"

"I was just thinking of them. His diary didn't say he was sorry exactly, but he was uneasy. That's something. His letter acknowledged some degree of guilt, and in it he offered to help Robert Taylor. I treated that letter pretty lightly when you read it out, but it would have been a landmark if Taylor had received it. Did he? He says not."

"He may have forgotten or be lying."

"Quite possibly—or his rooming house might have lost it. But when I asked you if you thought your father had sent it, you didn't venture an opinion. Was it because you couldn't be sure? Digby Watt had a decent impulse when he wrote the letter to Taylor. What did he do with that impulse? If he squashed it—if he trampled on his own best nature—I'd rather he'd never written those words at all. Can you tell me now, in so many words, 'If he wrote it, he mailed it'?"

"You know, I don't much care for being put on the spot."

"At least now you know how it feels."

"What does it matter if he mailed it?"

"It bears on your question which bears, I guess, on whether I see you again."

A couple of things hit me now, late in the game. I had banked too heavily on a rich girl's sense of fair play—that was for starters. And besides, it was too soon after her father's death to be talking about any of this.

"Better not," said Edith.

I stole a kiss from that perfect mouth of hers and walked away with as much nonchalance as my tingling lips left me across the broad lawn for the second and last time. I later read she had married a Russian count.

Acknowledgements

Loving thanks to Carol Jackson, the first and most frequent reader of this novel in manuscript. Her suggestions have helped me write a better book. For outstanding professional advice, I am indebted to Lesley Mann and Robert Ward. Photographer Elspeth Wood kindly advised me regarding the chemicals of her art. And RendezVous Press has once again been a pleasure to work with. To publisher Sylvia McConnell, editor Allister Thompson and marketing manager Adria Iwasutiak—merci.

Photo by Brett Newsome

Mel Bradshaw's previous novel *Death in the Age of Steam* (RendezVous Press, 2004) saw 1850s Canada through the eyes of a bank cashier turned amateur detective by the disappearance of a woman he once courted. The novel was shortlisted for an Arthur Ellis Award by the Crime Writers of Canada in the category of best first novel and won the American award, *Foreword* Magazine's Best Novel of the year, in the mystery genre. *Queen's Quarterly, Impulse, Descant,* and *The Dalhousie Review* are among the journals that have published Mel's short stories, most crime-related. He has also written on military history for *The Canadian Forum.*

Mel was born and grew up in Toronto, where he took his B.A. and was film editor of *The Varsity*. He holds a post-graduate degree in philosophy from Oxford University. His non-writing career is teaching English, which he has done in Canada and Southeast Asia. He has also travelled to Zambia, Iceland, Poland, and points between. He currently lives in his native town.

Praise for Mel Bradshaw's first novel, *Death in the Age of Steam*

"[an] exceptionally good first novel ..meandering story of love and death... Bradshaw keeps the reader firmly on the pavement with sights, sounds, smells and vivid descriptions of Victorian Canadian life... Banker Isaac Harris is only one of several beautifully crafted characters."
-The Globe and Mail

"...engrossing...Mel Bradshaw has created a novel that is very hard to put down."
-The Edmonton Journal

"Bradshaw has achieved a particular kind of literary feat... This is not merely a detective story in period dress, but a carefully constructed and exquisitely sketched novel of manners... It is a rich holiday treat which gives an insight into a city that often forgets it has a past: a visit to a lost world."
-Graham Fraser, *The Toronto Star*

"...meatier than many mysteries...with psychological depth and an acute sense of time and place, this book calls for slow savouring...greed, adultery, conspiracy, murder, and finally, love are as present in the nuclear age as the age of steam. This is not light reading, but a book well worth the time."
-Foreword Magazine

"...a meticulously researched portrait of the times...The novel moves toward an exciting and plausible conclusion...a delightful romance, mystery and detective story, full of history and brimming with intelligent and superbly-rendered characters."
-W.P. Kinsella, *Books in Canada*

"...the world resurrected by Bradshaw is nothing short of awe-inspiring. Throw in a well-constructed plot, a handful of sympathetic characters and a good love interest, and you've got an engaging mystery."
-The Montreal Gazette

Printed in the USA
CPSIA information can be obtained
at www.ICGtesting.com
JSHW082159140824
68134JS00014B/328